## "You're free," Constance said.

They were barely an inch apart from one another, so close that their breaths mixed and became one.

All sorts of things were going on inside of James. Things he couldn't understand or unravel. Things he felt it best not to examine.

"Not hardly," he murmured, more to himself than to her.

Constance's heart jumped up into her throat and made itself a home there just beneath the oval of the cameo.

And then everything stopped.

For all she knew, the world had abruptly stopped turning on its axis. Because she felt the room tilting.

James placed the crook of his finger beneath her chin and raised her head a fraction. Placing her lips just within reach.

Their eyes met and held. Seconds were knitting themselves into eternity.

She wasn't sure who cut the tiny distance between them to nothing....

Dear Reader,

If you're eagerly anticipating holiday gifts we can start you off on the right foot, with six compelling reads by authors established and new. Consider it a somewhat early Christmas, Chanukah or Kwanzaa present!

The gifting begins with another in *USA TODAY* bestselling author Susan Mallery's DESERT ROGUES series. In *The Sheik and the Virgin Secretary* a spurned assistant decides the only way to get over a soured romance is to start a new one—with her prince of a boss (literally). Crystal Green offers the last installment of MOST LIKELY TO... with *Past Imperfect,* in which we finally learn the identity of the secret benefactor—as well as Rachel James's parentage. Could the two be linked? In *Under the Mistletoe,* Kristin Hardy's next HOLIDAY HEARTS offering, a by-the-book numbers cruncher is determined to liquidate a grand New England hotel...until she meets the handsome hotel manager determined to restore it to its glory days—and capture her heart in the process! Don't miss *Her Special Charm,* next up in Marie Ferrarella's miniseries THE CAMEO. This time the finder of the necklace is a gruff New York police detective—surely he can't be destined to find love with its Southern belle of an owner, can he? In *Diary of a Domestic Goddess* by Elizabeth Harbison, a woman who is close to losing her job, her dream house and her livelihood finds she might be able to keep all three—*if* she can get close to her hotshot new boss who's annoyingly irresistible. And please welcome brand-new author Loralee Lillibridge—her debut book, *Accidental Hero,* features a bad boy come home, this time with scars, an apology—and a determination to win back the woman he left behind!

So celebrate! We wish all the best of everything this holiday season and in the New Year to come.

Happy reading,

Gail Chasan
Senior Editor

Please address questions and book requests to:
Silhouette Reader Service
U.S.: 3010 Walden Ave., P.O. Box 1325, Buffalo, NY 14269
Canadian: P.O. Box 609, Fort Erie, Ont. L2A 5X3

# HER SPECIAL CHARM
## MARIE FERRARELLA

Silhouette®

**SPECIAL EDITION**®

Published by Silhouette Books

America's Publisher of Contemporary Romance

To everyone who's ever believed,
against all odds, in the power of love.

 SILHOUETTE BOOKS

ISBN 0-373-24726-5

HER SPECIAL CHARM

Copyright © 2005 by Marie Rydzynski Ferrarella

This edition published by arrangement with Harlequin Books S.A.

® and TM are trademarks of Harlequin Books S.A., used under license.
Trademarks indicated with ® are registered in the United States Patent
and Trademark Office, the Canadian Trade Marks Office and in other
countries.

Visit Silhouette Books at www.eHarlequin.com

**Printed in U.S.A.**

## Books by Marie Ferrarella

**ChildFinders, Inc.**
*A Hero for All Seasons* IM #932
*A Forever Kind of Hero* IM #943
*Hero in the Nick of Time* IM #956
*Hero for Hire* IM #1042
*An Uncommon Hero*
  Silhouette Books
*A Hero in Her Eyes* IM #1059
*Heart of a Hero* IM #1105

**The Baby of the Month Club**
*Baby's First Christmas* SE #997
*Happy New Year—Baby!* IM #686
*The 7lb., 2oz. Valentine* Yours Truly
*Husband: Optional* SD #988
*Do You Take This Child?* SR #1145
*Detective Dad* World's Most
  Eligible Bachelors
*The Once and Future
  Father* IM #1017
*In the Family Way* Silhouette Books
*Baby Talk* Silhouette Books
*An Abundance of Babies* SE #1422

**The Bachelors of Blair Memorial**
*In Graywolf's Hands* IM #1155
*M.D. Most Wanted* IM #1167
*Mac's Bedside Manner* SE #1492
*Undercover M.D.* IM #1191
*The M.D.'s Surprise
  Family* SE #1653

**The Cameo**
*Because a Husband Is
  Forever* SE #1671
*She's Having a Baby* SE #1713
*Her Special Charm* SE #1726

*Unflashed series

**Those Sinclairs**
*Holding Out for a Hero* IM #496
*Heroes Great and Small* IM #501
*Christmas Every Day* IM #538
*Caitlin's Guardian Angel* IM #661

**The Cutlers of the Shady Lady Ranch**
(Yours Truly titles)
*Fiona and the Sexy Stranger*
*Cowboys Are for Loving*
*Will and the Headstrong Female*
*The Law and Ginny Marlow*
*A Match for Morgan*
*A Triple Threat to
  Bachelorhood* SR #1564

**\*The Alaskans**
*Wife in the Mail* SE #1217
*Stand-In Mom* SE #1294
*Found: His Perfect Wife* SE #1310
*The M.D. Meets His Match* SE #1401
*Lily and the Lawman* SE #1467
*The Bride Wore Blue Jeans* SE #1565

**The Mom Squad**
*A Billionaire and a Baby* SE #1528
*A Bachelor and a Baby* SD #1503
*The Baby Mission* IM #1220
*Beauty and the Baby* SR #1668

**Cavanaugh Justice**
*Racing Against Time* IM #1249
*Crime and Passion* IM #1256
*Internal Affair* Silhouette Books
*Dangerous Games* IM #1274
*The Strong Silent Type* SE #1613
*Cavanaugh's Woman* SE #1617
*In Broad Daylight* IM #1315
*Alone in the Dark* IM #1327
*Dangerous Disguise* IM #1339

# MARIE FERRARELLA

This *USA TODAY* bestselling and RITA® Award-winning author has written over 140 books for Silhouette, some under the name Marie Nicole. Her romances are beloved by fans worldwide.

*October 8, 1861*

*My dearest love,*

*I hope this letter finds you and that you are well and whole. That is the worst of this awful war, the not knowing where you are and if you are. I tell myself that in my heart, I would know if you are no longer among the living. That if you were taken from me in body as well as in spirit, some piece of my heart would surely wither and die because it only beats for you.*

*Each evening I press a kiss to my fingers and touch the cameo you gave me—the very same one I shall not remove until you are standing right here beside me—and pray that in the morning I will rise and look out my window to see you coming over the ridge. It is what sustains me in these dark hours.*

*I miss you and love you more each day.*

*Your Amanda*

## *Prologue*

*July 1, 1865*

Amanda Deveaux paused to wipe her forehead with the back of her hand. The sun was merciless today. As merciless as the war that had engulfed them all these long years, turning all their lives into ashes.

She paused and looked to the north. To the road that led onto her property. She hoped to see some sign of Will. Like every day since he had left her to fight and be brave, there was no sign of his approach.

Amanda sighed. Each day her hope grew a little thinner, her despair a little heavier.

Squaring her shoulders, she wrapped her fingers

around the hoe she'd been using to coax life from the garden that sustained them.

The War between the States had come to an end three months ago, but not her ordeal. That continued to stretch out endlessly before her, each day no different than the one before. No different than the one after.

Everything had changed since Lt. William Slattery had ridden away, leaving her behind to wait. To pray. To each day slip a little further into her own personal living hell. The war had taken her brother Jonathan. He was one of the many who had fallen at Chancellorsville. And it had taken her father as well. Not on the battlefield, but here, where each day she watched him grow more distant, more lost. Eventually, Alexander Deveaux had faded away from life because his oldest born was no longer in it.

A year ago, her younger sister, Susannah, had married Frasier O'Brien. Frasier had come home early from the war, nursing a wound, and had just forgotten to return. He'd taken over his father's emporium, sustaining the town at a large profit to himself. Savannah had become his wife and avarice his mistress, which suited her mother just fine. Belinda Deveaux admired a man who worshipped money. Which was why her mother had never liked Will. His family's wealth had never met her standards.

And now, no one but Frasier had money.

She knew her mother had been secretly glad when Will's name had appeared on that awful list of men who were missing. That had been almost two years ago.

Right after Gettysburg had broken their backs and their spirit.

Many had left the area, but even after her father had died, Amanda continued working the plantation with the few emancipated souls who had chosen to stay in the only home they had ever known. She couldn't pay them. They remained anyway, saying that when there was money to be had, they would collect.

And all the while, she watched the road, praying for some sign of the man she had never stopped loving. The man whose cameo she wore around her neck, the one she had promised never to remove until he returned to claim her for his bride.

The ivory image of Penelope against the Wedgwood-blue background had been worn down from her constant fingering. She touched it whenever she thought of Will. And whenever she prayed for his safe return.

She touched it a great deal.

In town, they called her "the widow woman who had never been a wife" behind her back. They said she was a little crazy, waiting for a dead man to come back to her.

She didn't care what people said. All she cared about was getting from one end of the day to the other, holding on until Will returned to her. Because he had given his word that he would and he had never broken a promise to her.

Amanda got back to work. There were mouths to feed and people depending on her.

# Chapter One

*Present Day.*

James Munro liked to come out early in the morning, when the city that never slept dozed a little. At five-thirty in the morning, New York City was a little less. A little less noisy, a little less traffic and, the elements willing, a little less sweltering. So far, July had been merciless.

So he and his dog Stanley went out to jog earlier and earlier, trying to find some kind of happy medium between exercising and melting in the heat of the morning. It was the only time of day when he could make his mind a blank. To focus on nothing. To keep away the demons that populated his world.

The air was particularly hard to draw into his lungs this morning. Just a little farther, he promised himself as he sprinted from one curb to the next, and then he and Stanley could turn around and go home.

He'd turn at the newsstand on the next corner. The way he always did. Raul, the man who operated the tiny stand, was usually just opening up as he'd make his turn. They had a nodding acquaintance. More than once, Raul looked as if he wanted to say something. But the ex-vet, as the sign over the newsstand proudly proclaimed, could save it for one of his customers, James thought. He wasn't out here to talk to anyone. Except maybe Stanley.

He didn't see the woman until he'd almost tripped over her.

Which was highly unusual, given that, as a robbery-and-burglary detective, James was pretty much aware of all his surroundings, even when he was tuning things out. But one minute, there was no one in front of him, and the next, he had to come to a skidding halt to avoid colliding with the short, rounded woman in the soft-blue sundress.

Reflexes honed to a sharp point, James just narrowly avoided running straight into her. Stanley, his five-year-old German shepherd, looked disgruntled as he shifted from side to side, wanting to continue.

The jog was placed on hold. Thrown off balance, the woman sank to the sidewalk right in front of James. His arms went out to break her fall, but he was too late. She was already down. For a second, James was convinced he was going to have to summon an ambulance. People around the woman's apparent age didn't fall like that without suffering consequences.

A startled, small cry escaped from the woman's lips as she met the concrete, but there was no scream, no cry of anguish. There wasn't even a look of horror flashing across her cherubic face.

Stanley tossed his noble head, barking once, as if to bring James's attention to the woman on the sidewalk. The dog's keen brown eyes darted around. Stanley had obviously appointed himself the woman's guardian until such time as his master helped her to her feet and they could be back on their way.

The woman attempted to rise. "No, wait," James cautioned, placing a hand on her shoulder, "don't try to get up."

She gave him a kindly, if reproving, glare. "I can't just sit here all day, young man. At my age, it isn't dignified. Besides, in half an hour I'll be in everyone's way." She extended her hand to him, a patient expression on her face.

He had no choice but to help her up. Placing one arm around her shoulders, he all but lifted her to her feet and was surprised at how light she felt. She gained her feet a little uncertainly, but seemed determined to stand.

James had his doubts about what she was doing. She had to be seventy-five if she was a day. "Are you sure you're all right?"

The woman waved away his concern. "I'm fine, young man, really. Just a little bruised and winded. And embarrassed," she added in a lowered tone that ended in a small chuckle.

James stifled the urge to brush the woman off. The last robbery victim he and his partner, Nick Santini, had interviewed was about this woman's age. The interview had been conducted in a hospital because the woman had suffered a heart attack during the robbery. "No reason for that. I came up on you suddenly."

She smiled warmly at him. "That you did. I was counting out my change for the newspaper." She nodded toward the stand at the end of the block, then her bright blue eyes turned toward the German shepherd standing beside him. Stanley was panting audibly, his tongue almost touching the sidewalk. "He won't bite me, will he?"

For a dog whose mother had been a guard dog, Stanley had turned out to be incredibly docile. "Not unless you're committing a felony."

"Oh my, no." The woman covered her mouth with her steepled fingers, as if to keep her smile from widening too much and splitting her face. And then her eyes took full measure of him. He could almost feel her thinking. "You're a policeman, aren't you?"

Since he was wearing sweats that proclaimed a popular line of clothing rather than tying him in with any particular precinct, he was a little taken aback by her question. "How would you know that?"

Her smile was disarming. "Just something about your bearing." Her eyes swept over him. "I can always tell." And then, after a beat, she added, "My son Michael was a policeman."

She said the words with pride. But she'd used the past tense. Though when he was outside the job, he didn't usually possess any curiosity, James still heard himself asking, "Was?"

She nodded. "He retired." And then she frowned slightly, but it wasn't the kind of frown that bore malice or any ill feelings at all. She shivered, as if to throw off her earlier words. "Makes me feel old, saying that. Thought it was bad enough when my husband retired, but now I have a retired son as well."

Her eyes seemed to delve into his as she spoke. Being a good detective had taught him how to listen, even when there wasn't anything worth listening to, as this clearly wasn't. It had no place in the small world around him.

"He lives out in Arizona. Don't see him and his family nearly as much we both would like. If Michael were here, I would give this to him to take care of."

She hadn't hit her head, but maybe the fall had jarred something loose anyway. James hadn't the slightest idea what she was talking about. "'This'?"

"The necklace."

It was just getting stranger. He shook his head, wondering if she knew Raul. He could leave her at the newspaper stand and Raul could take care of her. He shifted his body, ready to lead her over to the man. "I'm sorry, ma'am, but I don't quite…"

She pointed to the ground. "Right there, at your feet. It's what caught my attention while I was counting my change. I didn't see you coming at all."

Looking down to humor her, James didn't expect to see anything.

But there is was.

An old-fashioned piece of jewelry from the looks of it. It was attached to a black velvet ribbon that was no longer tied together. Stooping down to pick it up, he held the cameo up to the woman.

"It's not yours?"

A delicate hand fluttered to her ample bosom. "Oh my, no. Wish it was." And then she smiled. "My memory's not that bad, young man. Still remember what happened to me years ago. And minutes ago," she added with a twinkle in her eye.

Leaning forward, the woman looked at the cameo she'd pointed out. Stanley came forward and did the same, sniffing the piece, or perhaps the black velvet ribbon that was attached to it. James was tempted to ask Stanley if he detected the scent of past owners on it.

"Lovely, isn't it?" the woman suddenly asked him. "Exquisite, really. And expensive, I'd say. Probably has a history to it. Perhaps a family heirloom." She raised her eyes to his. "Someone must be very upset about losing it." She said it as if it were an emphatic statement that left no room for argument. "I'd say the best thing you could do would be to place an ad in the newspaper about it." She put her hand over his. "It would be the kind thing to do, putting an end to someone's unrest."

It might be the kind thing to do, but in his line of work, there was no room for kindness, no time to stop and even notice the roses, much less attempt to smell one of them.

He opened his mouth to say as much.

James couldn't explain it. If he tried, he was sure whoever he told would think he was crazy. Maybe he even entertained that notion himself, but when the old woman placed her small, soft hand on his, he experienced the oddest sensation of peace wafting over him. Something he was completely unacquainted with, but somehow still recognized.

It was fleeting, but it was there.

He cleared his throat, giving a half shrug. "Maybe I'll do that."

She beamed with pride, looking every inch the grandmother than he had never known.

"That's just what I'd expect an officer of the law to say." She glanced at the piece, than back at him. "It's a cameo, you know."

"No," he admitted, "I didn't." Santini knew his way around jewelry, but he didn't. The man's wife demanded a decent piece for every occasion.

"Young men don't usually," the woman replied with a gentle laugh. Taking the cameo from him for a moment, she turned it around to examine. "And there seems to be an inscription on it." Her eyes squinted. "But it's very faint."

He took it from her and looked at the back of the cameo. At first, there appeared to be nothing, but when he angled it just right, the early New York sun bounced off it in a way that managed to highlight very faint, thin letters.

"From W.S. to A.D.," he read out loud.

He supposed she was right. This was more than just a piece of junk jewelry. Still, he would have paid it no mind if the woman hadn't pointed it out to him. His field might be robbery, but his expertise was the criminal mind. When it came to things like jewelry, he didn't know costume from the real thing. That was for someone else to ascertain.

If he put an ad in the paper, phone calls would start coming in and he didn't have the time or, more to the point, the desire to interact with the callers this would bring out of the woodwork. That kind of thing was for someone who didn't have a life that went full throttle every waking minute.

He turned to the woman, holding out the cameo to her. "I think that maybe you should be the one who places the ad in the paper. After all, you're the one who really found it."

James fully expected her to take the cameo from him. So he was surprised when she placed both her hands over his, closing his hand around the piece of jewelry, and shook her head.

"No, my dear, I think that you would be better suited for the task," she pronounced softly, her voice carrying the kind of conviction he found very difficult to argue against.

But he was nothing if not firm. He just didn't have the time for this. "No, I—"

"Trust me," she said, her eyes on his. "I have an instinct about these things."

He frowned. Just what the city needed, another pseudo-psychic. Still, in his experience, people usually were quick to take what wasn't theirs. That she didn't was admirable.

"If no one claims this, it's yours, you know."

"Yes," she murmured, looking down at the cameo in his palm. "I know."

Well, if he had to do this, he might as well get to it. Time and his early morning were ticking away. "Why don't you give me your name and address and your telephone number—"

There was pleasure in the woman's eyes as she laughed. He was struck by the thought that she must have been beautiful at one point. And that time was a thief. "Anyone listening would say you were asking me for a date. My name is Harriet. Harriet Stewart. I live just over there, in those apartments."

She pointed vaguely toward a block that was comprised of two high-rise buildings standing elbow to elbow as they faced the early morning haze.

Stanley was impatient to be gone. That made two of them, James thought. By now, he would have been more than halfway through his jog and back to his apartment for a quick shower and another regenerating cup of black coffee before he went to the precinct.

This woman with her pleasant chatter was throwing everything off. "You're going to have to be more specific than that."

"Wait, I'll write it down for you." Taking a piece of paper and a pen out of her purse, Harriet quickly jotted down the particulars, then handed him the paper. "And you're with the fifty-first, right?"

He looked at her, the hairs on the back of his neck beginning to stand at attention, the way they always did when something was out of sync. He'd never met this woman before. He would have remembered if he had. "How would you know that?"

She gave a slight shrug of her shoulders. "Closest one here. A detective likes to live near his precinct. Makes rushing to the scene of the crime in the middle of the night easier."

When she said this, it sounded humorous, not suspicious. Probably something her son had told her at one time or another, James thought.

"Yeah, right." Because there was no other choice available to him if he wanted to get going, he closed his hand over the cameo.

"You have to go," she said with an understanding nod of her head.

"Yeah, I do." He muttered something that passed for "Goodbye," then turned toward his dog. "Let's go, Stanley."

"Don't lose the cameo," Harriet called after him cheerfully as he began to jog away from her.

James sighed. "I won't."

He could have sworn that Stanley sighed right along with him.

"You mean she wasn't hot?" Disappointment dripped from Detective Nicholas Santini's every pore as he stared at his partner within their police vehicle.

James had no idea why he'd said anything at all to

Santini. It wasn't as if he was one for sharing. That was Santini's department. Santini shared everything with him, from last night's fight with Rita to his concern with premature male-pattern baldness—something anyone looking at the man's extremely full head of hair would have chalked off to paranoia. James was the closed-mouth one, but the woman he'd encountered had left a strange impression on him and he guessed he just wanted to sound it out loud.

His mistake. Santini was like a dog with a bone. A starving dog.

James sighed as he drove down the corner. The light had just turned red. He *hated* waiting for the light to change. "She looked to be about seventy-five, Santini. Maybe a seventy-six-year-old would have found her hot, but no, she wasn't hot."

Santini shook his head. "First woman you trip over—" he slanted a glance at his partner of three years "—literally—in I don't know how long and she has to turn out to be a senior citizen." The dark, weathered face gathered around a pout. "Couldn't you have run into a hot babe?"

James thought of the cameo he'd left locked up in his desk drawer at home. He still had to place the ad and he was dreading the deluge of response he anticipated. "I wasn't trying to run into anyone and if your wife catches you talking like that, you'll be sleeping on the screened porch again." The light turned green and he was off.

Santini jolted, then settled back. After three years, he

still wasn't accustomed to the fits and starts of his partner's driving.

"Yeah, I know. But a guy can dream, can't he? I can't step out on her—won't step out on her," Santini amended, probably because the former sounded as if he were henpecked, which he had admitted in a moment laced with weakness and whiskey, but it wasn't something he liked dwelling on, "but I can live through you—if you had a life, that is." He frowned deeply, forming ruts around the corners of his mouth. "You owe it to me, Munro."

He took another corner, sharply. Santini moaned beside him. "Watching your back is all I owe you, Santini."

Santini shifted in his seat, his hand braced against the glove compartment. Another turn was coming up. "So, you putting in the ad?"

It wasn't something he wanted to do, but Harriet Stewart was right. Someone was undoubtedly upset over losing a piece like this. The more he looked at it, the prettier it became. He could almost see it sitting against someone's throat, moving with every breath she took.

He blinked, wondering if the heat was getting to him. Even the air-conditioning in the car was struggling with the air. "At lunchtime."

Patience had never been Santini's long suit. "Why don't you do it now?"

James snorted. "In case you haven't noticed, we've got a crime scene to cover."

Responsibilities had shifted when it came to locking up crime scenes. These days, the scientists seemed to be all over it before the detectives had a chance even to survey the scene. "Why don't you let the CSU guys do our walking for us? Most of the time they get all huffy if we're in their 'way.'"

It was a constant battle for supremacy. Each department felt they had dibs on solving crimes. It hadn't been this way in his uncle's day, when detectives were gods—or so his uncle liked to tell. "And what, hold on to this job with my looks?"

Santini considered for a long moment, then shook his head. "Naw, couldn't happen. You'd be let go in five minutes."

"Not before you, Santini," he said, taking a quick turn and then pulling the car up short. Santini nearly bounced in his seat. "Not before you."

Just as he'd predicted. One look at his answering machine and he saw he was drowning in phone calls.

He glanced at the glaring red number. Fifteen. Fifteen callers since the ad had appeared this morning, each probably purporting to own the cameo. He sat down and played them all.

Only one was a hang-up, signifying a telemarketer. The rest of the calls were from people who claimed that the cameo belonged to them. Didn't take a Solomon to know that at least thirteen if not all fourteen were lying.

He frowned as the last message ended and a metallic voice came on to say, "End of final message."

"Might as well get this over with." The words were addressed to the dog who had come to greet him when he'd opened the front door.

James opened up a can of dog food for Stanley, took out a bottle of beer from the refrigerator for himself and settled into his recliner with a pad and pencil to return the calls.

The claims were all bogus, down to the last number on the answering machine. A great many of the stories had been creative as to how the cameo had been lost, but no one could tell him about the faint inscription etched on the back of the cameo.

A couple of the people he called back had figured out that it wasn't an inscription but initials, but as to what those initials were, they claimed to draw a blank, saying it had been so long since they'd looked at the back, they couldn't remember. He told them to call back when they regained their memory.

"Incredible city we live in," he murmured to the dog as he hung up on the last caller. "Give them a crisis and they all pull together. Dangle a piece of jewelry in front of them and it's every man or woman for themselves."

James sighed and shook his head. He'd never been a great believer in the nobility of man to begin with, but he hated being proven right. Getting up, he took his empty bottle to the garbage.

As he dropped it in, he saw the dog eyeing him. "Yeah, yeah, I know, I should be recycling, but I don't have the time. If you're so hot on the issue, you go and recycle them."

Stanley just continued looking at him with his big, soulful brown eyes.

James blew out a breath, dug the bottle out of the garbage and put it on the side. "C'mon, I need a jog. Maybe it'll clear my head." And then he grinned. "Maybe we'll trip over a diamond this time. Or a 'hot babe.'" He used Santini's words for the experience. "If we do, we'll put her on Santini's doorstep, see what his wife has to say about it. You with me?"

Stanley barked in response.

"Good dog."

He went to change out of his clothes and into his jogging shorts and shirt.

Forty-five minutes later, he was back, dripping. The humidity that held the city hostage seemed to have gone up a notch as the sun went down instead of relinquishing its grip. It was like trying to run through minestrone soup.

Throwing his keys on the table, he saw the blinking light.

Another call.

"Well, it can keep," he told his dog, pouring fresh cold water for him into a bowl. Stanley began to lap as if he hadn't had a drink in seven drought-filled days. "I need a shower."

The light was still blinking seductively at him after he came out of the shower.

And while he ate a dinner comprised of a ham sandwich. He eyed the hypnotic light as he chewed, toying with the idea of just deleting it without listening, or at least putting it off until morning.

Greed always left a bad taste in his mouth and the slew of people he'd encountered this evening, all wanting something for nothing, had put him off. Bad enough he encountered it every day on the job, people stealing the sweat of someone else's brow, absconding with someone's dream when they had no right to it. But he damn well didn't have to welcome it with open arms right here on his own turf.

But he knew that wasn't strictly the case.

"Wrong, Munro. You put the ad in, you opened the floodgates. Now take your medicine."

Mercifully, there was only one message on his machine. He pressed down the button, bracing himself.

The voice that slipped into his humidity-laced third-floor apartment reminded him of warm brandy being poured over honey. It was soft, with more than a hint of a Southern accent.

The voice made him sit up and listen.

"My name is Constance Beaulieu. I believe you've found my mother's cameo, sir."

*Chapter Two*

James shifted on the sofa, moving a little closer to the coffee table—and the phone—as he listened to the woman on his answering machine.

"The cameo has great sentimental value, sir, especially now that my mother's passed on. Please call me at your earliest convenience. I'll be on pins and needles until I hear from you." She left her number and then offered a melodic, almost inviting, "Bye," before the connection was broken.

He didn't realize that he'd been holding his breath until he was compelled to release it. Listening to Constance Beaulieu had the same effect as walking through a field filled with honeysuckle blossoms. His head felt as if it were spinning.

James glanced at Stanley. Sitting at his feet, the dog gave every indication that he had been listening just as intently as James had. He cleared his throat. "Lays it on rather thick, doesn't she?"

Stanley turned his head in his master's direction. For once, there was no response from the animal.

James blew out a long breath, shaking himself free of whatever it was that had just transpired. Undoubtedly a reaction to the long day he'd put in and the heat that was lingering over the city like a heavy, oppressive hand pushing its citizens down to the ground.

"You're not buying this 'my-mother-passed-on' bit, are you, Stanley?" He snorted. "Oldest ploy in the world. And that accent—I'll bet you a steak dinner she's really from Brooklyn."

This time, Stanley did bark, as if to tell him that they were on. James already knew that Stanley would do absolutely anything for steak. The dog was too damn spoiled.

"Right, and if I win, you have to try that healthy dog food you keep snubbing." Stanley just looked at him with eyes that could have been either mournful or intuitive, depending on his own mood. "Okay, you're on."

Might as well get this one over with as well, he thought. Pulling the telephone over to himself, James began to tap out the phone number she'd left on the answering machine.

Part of him felt it was just another wild goose chase. But he was a cop through and through. Doing the right thing was what he was all about. Even if doing the right thing meant putting up with a lot of wrong people. Hitting the last number, he braced himself.

The phone barely rang once before he heard the receiver being snatched up on the other end.

"Hello?"

The single breathlessly uttered word echoed seductively in his ear. As it took the long way around to his brain cells, an image arose in his head of long, cool limbs, blond hair that moved like a silken curtain in the breeze and a mouth that was, to quote Goldilocks, "Just right."

He cleared his throat, wishing he could clear his mind as well. Maybe Santini was right. Maybe what he needed was a woman. Not for a relationship or even any kind of a long-term companionship, but just for the most basic, mutual physical satisfaction. "Is this Constance Beaulieu?"

"Yes." Another image flashed through his mind. A Christmas tree, standing in the middle of a darkened room, being plugged in and suddenly flooding the same area with light. "Are you James?"

He wasn't too keen on the familiar tone her voice had taken. "I'm James."

Honeyed words slowly poured over him, one following the other, giving him no opportunity to say anything beyond that.

"And you have my cameo. I can't tell you how very relieved I am. I'd just about given up hope of ever seeing it again. It's been missing for more than a year now. It was stolen—"

He thought he perceived her taking a breath. He took his opportunity where he could and jumped in with both feet before she got her second wind. "Well, before you get all relieved, Ms. Beaulieu—"

"Constance," she corrected.

James suppressed a sigh. "Before you get all relieved, Ms. Beaulieu," he repeated. He was aware of the old confidence trick aimed at disarming the would-be mark by creating a warm, friendly atmosphere. That wasn't about to happen. Not if he was the so-called mark. "I'd like you to describe the cameo to me."

He expected her to pause. Instead, she sounded pleased that he'd actually asked.

"Of course. It's a profile of a lady. Her hair is all piled up on her head. She's ivory colored and she's up against a background of Wedgwood-blue. The same color of the original owner's eyes," she added just when he thought she was finished.

Nice touch, he thought. But the description just might have been a lucky guess. According to what Santini had told him, a lot of cameos had Wedgwood-blue backgrounds. She was going to have to do better than that if she wanted him to hand over the necklace to her. He turned it over in his hand, looking at the back.

"Tell me something that's not in the ad," he instructed tersely.

There was a pause on the other end. When it continued, he thought he had her. She was like the rest, an opportunist. Too bad. This one had imagination. And style.

Not that he bought into the Southern accent, that was a little over the top, but—

"There's an inscription on the back."

Her soft voice, burrowing into his thoughts, caught him off guard. "What?"

"Well, not really an inscription," she corrected herself. "More like initials. Faint ones. You might not even be able to make them out unless you hold them up to the light, just right. But if you do, you'll see that it reads From W.S to A.D. The A.D. stands for Amanda Deveaux. She's my great-times-seven grandmother," she clarified.

He could have sworn he heard a smile in the woman's voice. She had to be pulling his leg with this. But if so, how did she know about the initials? That *wasn't* a lucky guess. "Excuse me?"

He heard a small chuckle. At his expense? "It's easier saying great-times-seven than stretching it out and saying great-great-great-great—"

"I get the picture," he told her gruffly. He looked at the cameo he'd placed on the coffee table. "I guess it's yours, all right."

He thought he heard a little squeal of joy, but that could have just been the phone line, crackling. Nonetheless, the sound zipped through him.

"I appreciate you taking such precautions, James. I can come over right now and pick it up. There's a reward, of course. It's not much, but—"

Again, he cut her short. "I don't want any reward. I'm a cop." Ironically, since he worked in R&B, robbery and burglary, this fit nicely into his job description. "This is all part of what I do."

"A policeman." This time, the little laugh that left her lips somehow managed to shimmy up his spine. And, much to his annoyance, move in for the duration of the phone call. "New York's finest. I should have known."

He frowned. She'd lost him. "Known what?"

"That if anyone would have reported finding it, it had to be someone honorable."

He didn't know how well that description fit him. There were times, when he and Santini were chasing down a so-called suspect, someone who took rather than earned and beat anyone who got in his way, that he found himself toying with the notion of taking the law into his own hands. Of going that extra step and making the felon pay for his crimes without dragging the court system and their endless delays into it.

At bottom, he knew that way was anarchy, so he had never acted upon his rare impulses. Still, it was exceedingly tempting to turn thought into reality….

"So," the woman on the other end of his telephone was saying, "if you'll just give me your address, I can be over within the hour, depending on where you live, if that's all right with you."

No, it wasn't all right with him. It was so far from all right with him that there was no human way to chart it. Giving out his address was something he rarely did. The department knew where he lived. So did his ex-wife, although with her being in California, he doubted if that made a difference.

But aside from key members of the department, and Eli Levy, the old man who ran the mom-and-pop store he frequented, no one else knew where he lived. He was as private a man as possible in this age of information invasion. And it was going to remain that way.

"Why don't you come down to the precinct tomorrow?" The suggestion was said in such a way that it clearly wasn't a suggestion at all but an order. "I'll have it for you then. Say nine o'clock?"

He heard a slight hesitation on the other end, as if she were torn over something. "I have to be in school at nine."

"You're a student?"

"No," she laughed, ushering in another shiver. "I'm a teacher."

He listened to his air-conditioning unit struggling. "But this is summer," he pointed out.

"It's an all-year school," she told him. "Is four o'clock all right?"

Never would be better, he thought, but he'd gotten himself into this. The sooner it was over, the better everything would be. He and Santini had some canvassing to do involving the string of restaurant robberies they were investigating, but he could see to it that he was back at the precinct by four. Santini wouldn't object.

"Four o'clock," he echoed. "I'm at the fifty-first precinct."

He began to give her the address but she stopped him. "I know where that is."

He wondered if that meant she just passed it on a regular basis, or that she had firsthand dealings with one or more of the people there. Again, the thought of a confidence game came to mind. But if that was the case, she was one of the best scam artists he'd ever encountered. "Third floor. Ask for James Munro."

"Like the president."

Everyone said that. It took effort for him not to give in to irritation. Instead, he kept his temper in check. "Yeah, like the president. Except we spell the last name differently."

She surprised him by apologizing. "Sorry, you must hear that all the time."

There was that little laugh again. The one that sounded like bluebells ringing. The thought caught him up short. Since when did he wax poetic about anything, much less some stranger's voice on the phone? He was getting punchy. That last outing with Stanley in this heat had done him in.

"It's just that I'm so very excited."

She obviously meant that by way of an explanation. Why the words would suddenly nudge things around in his mind, forming close to erotic thoughts about a woman he had never even laid eyes on, he had no idea.

Despite all logic, a feeling vaguely akin to arousal slipped through him.

Annoyed with himself and the caller, he banked his reaction down immediately. Maybe Santini with all his talk of available women and how he should be out there was seeping into his subconscious.

Whatever the cause, he didn't like it. Didn't like not having complete control over every part of himself. Especially his mind.

"Tomorrow, then," he said. He was about to hang up, then a thought occurred to him. He didn't exactly have a nine-to-five job where he could be found in a given place at a given time. Circumstances did have a way of intervening. Because of that, though it was against his better judgment, he added, "Let me give you my cell number, just in case you get lost."

"I won't get lost, James," she said with the kind of confidence that came from self-awareness rather than bravado. "But I appreciate the offer."

Everything the woman said appealed to him. It took effort not to allow himself to be drawn in.

James fairly barked out the number at her, then quickly hung up before she could say anything further that would cause him to linger on the phone. He shook his head, not in disbelief but to get his bearings back.

As he banished the residue of the strange sensations that were still milling around him like morning mists on the moors, he became aware that Stanley was eyeing him with what appeared to be satisfaction, if such an emotion could have been attributed to a four-footed animal.

He knew what *that* was all about. In his opinion, Stanley was smarter than a lot of people he had to deal with.

"Okay," he sighed, "you win. Steak. Tomorrow." Stanley came closer and laid his head on James's lap.

He could feel the animal's warm breath on his thigh. "I'm not going to the store tonight so you can just back off, you hear me? Go stare down something else."

It turned out to be a Mexican standoff. James did manage to hold firm about his resolution not to go to the grocery store to buy the dog the promised steak tonight. However, unable to endure the animal's soulful, penetrating look for more than fifteen minutes, he'd wound up taking the chicken breast he'd meant for his own dinner out of the refrigerator and frying it up for the both of them.

The preponderance of the meal, as always, went to Stanley. The dog took it as his due.

It smelled faintly of cleaning products and the sweat of fear, despite the noble efforts of the less than powerful air-conditioning system struggling to make a difference against the oppressive weather outside.

Walking just inside the front door, Constance Beaulieu took a moment to absorb it all. She'd never been inside a police station before. Even when she'd called to report her mother's cameo stolen, two policemen had been sent to her to take down the information.

Privilege did that, she thought with a hint of a smile playing along her lips. That and the fact that her parents had been friends with New York's chief of police, the man she'd grown up calling Uncle Bob. The man who she believed, had her mother been so inclined, would have become her stepfather after her own father had passed away.

But her mother had been a one-man woman to her dying breath and Bob Wheeler had respected that, even as it killed him to do so.

Uncle Bob hadn't wanted either her or her mother to come down to the same place where addicts, prostitutes and known felons passed through. He'd been very adamant about that. She'd eventually turned her curiosity in other directions. Uncle Bob would have been unhappy with her if he'd found out she'd gone against his wishes. Like her mother, she loved the man dearly. Maybe a little more so as she'd grown up and realized just how much he'd given up to be there for them. The man had never married.

"Can I help you?" a male voice behind her asked.

Constance turned around to see a short, squat, powerful-looking man standing directly behind her. He made her think of a tag-team wrestler and gave the impression that he might break out of his rumpled jacket if he took too much of a deep breath.

Grateful for his help, she smiled at him. "I'm looking for Detective James Munro."

The man who was just a little taller than she was, but not by much, made no response. He looked at her as if she'd just declared she had come in from Mars and wanted to be taken to the leader of Earth for a conquering tour of the place.

Maybe he was embarrassed that he couldn't help, she thought. Not wanting to be responsible for putting the man on the spot, she gave a small shrug of her shoulder, indicating that it was no big deal. "I can just ask the desk sergeant if Detective Munro's in if you don't know him."

It took Santini a moment longer, but he found his tongue. It was right there, stuck to the roof of his mouth. He peeled it off, still struggling to absorb what seemed to be happening.

"Oh, I know him, all right." His blossoming grin threatened to take over his entire face. "At least, I thought I did until just now. And he's in," he assured her. "Just." They'd come back fifteen minutes ago. For no apparent reason, Munro had abruptly driven their vehicle back to the precinct, saying that he had to see about something.

This woman certainly qualified as "something," Santini thought. He shook his head. It was always the quiet ones who surprised you.

His eyes swept over her, issuing a silent compliment. The woman couldn't have been put together better if she'd been made to order according to the specs of someone's fantasy.

"This way," he prompted, leading her to the elevator. "I'll take you to him. And if you don't mind my saying it, now I understand what all the hurry was about."

She didn't mind him saying it. She just didn't understand what he was saying. "Hurry?"

They stepped into the elevator. The silver doors closed. "I'm Detective Nick Santini." Pressing for the third floor, he then put out his hand to her. He had to hand it to James. The man could certainly pick them. "James's partner. He might have mentioned me."

She didn't want to hurt his feelings, but could see no reason why the detective she was meeting would have felt the need to mention his partner at all. "No, I'm afraid he didn't."

To which Santini nodded. "On second thought, that sounds more like James."

Constance had no idea why the man who said he was James Munro's partner looked so much like a cat that had just stolen a bowl of cream, but she pretended not to notice during their short ride in the elevator.

When the tarnished silver doors opened on the third floor, James's partner indicated the direction she should take and then fell into step beside her.

"So, have you known James long?" he asked amiably.

Maybe the detective had her confused with someone else, she thought. "Oh, I don't know him at all."

Santini nodded sagely, or what he hoped would pass as sagely.

"Know exactly what you mean. Feels that way to me, too, sometimes. The man's like a human clam. If you ask me, I think Stanley gets the best of his conversation." Realizing that might just put her off, he quickly interjected, "But don't get me wrong, Munro's a good guy and a great detective. Nobody I'd rather have watch my back."

They took a corner in the narrow hallway. Santini was aware that the two detectives they passed looked at him with renewed interest because of his companion. "My wife says the same thing. There's none better, unless the only thing you're after is some decent conversation." And then he laughed as he opened the door to the squad room and held it for her. "But you probably already know that."

He was talking so fast, he was making her head spin. Though she'd lived in New York since she was fifteen and thought she'd gotten accustomed to the pace in the city, she still had trouble when it came to having words shot at her at the speed of light. There was no doubt about it. Yankees talked too fast.

Except for the man she'd spoken to on the phone last night. He marched to his own drummer, and the beat was a slow one. She rather liked that.

"No, I…"

Her voice drifted off as she looked around the large room. The area was broken up into cubicles, with names affixed just outside each entrance. In actuality, she had no idea what the man she was meeting looked like. From the sound of his voice and the sparse exchange they'd had, she guessed that he had to be in his thirties, possibly his forties.

She smiled to herself as she scanned the area. The man had sounded distant. And tall. She could have spared herself the search. Her newly self-appointed guide was off like a bloodhound that had caught the scent.

"There he is, over there."

He pointed to a tall, muscular man in a light blue shirt. The man's sleeves were rolled up and he had a weapon and holster strapped across his chest and back with a perspiration stain forming along the rim of the leather. He made her think of a warrior waiting for his next battle.

Santini raised his voice to get James's attention. "Munro, you devil, you've been holding out on me," he declared before he ever reached James.

The latter turned around, about to demand to know what the hell his partner was babbling about now, but the words became stuck in his throat before he ever got a chance to utter them.

He'd made the mistake of looking beyond his partner to the woman in Santini's wake.

The second he saw her, he knew.

This was the woman who'd called about the cameo.

She was the kind of woman who turned heads and now was no exception. As he glanced around the squad room, he saw that every set of eyes within the small space were firmly pinned to her as she made her way toward him.

Her smile was liquid seduction. He could almost feel every step she took vibrating inside of him, its tempo increasing.

He'd all but talked himself into believing that the woman with the silky voice undoubtedly resembled a troll-in-training. That kind of thing was nature's way of playing a little joke on him. The silky voice made you conjure up images of an impossibly beautiful woman only to shatter those images with harsh reality. The smoothest male voice he'd ever heard belonged to a man who was five-seven and weighed in at three hundred twenty pounds on his lightest day. There was no reason to assume that the same wouldn't be true for the cameo owner.

James realized that his powers of deduction were shot to hell.

## Chapter Three

For a moment, he felt as if he couldn't take his eyes off her. The woman's smile was warm, inviting. Radiant. Standing in its aura, a man could almost believe that people were naturally good instead of desperately in need of redemption.

No one had ever accused him of being talkative, but his mind never went blank—except for now. It didn't help matters any that every single person on the floor was looking at him with unabashed surprise, as well as a touch of envy.

His lack of visitors was a known fact. In his seven years at the precinct, he hadn't received so much as a personal phone call. Stanley didn't know how to dial the phone and there was no one else, if he didn't count Eli Levy. Which he didn't because Eli would never call here despite all the years they had known one another. Theirs was a one-on-one, eye-to-eye kind of relationship.

"Detective Munro."

On her lips, his name sounded almost like a song. Which was fitting because she moved toward him like a melody, her hand outstretched, her manner as welcoming as if this were her turf, not his. As if they were old friends instead of strangers.

After a beat, James realized that some sort of reciprocation on his part was necessary. Rousing himself, he took her hand and shook it. Soft, speculative murmurs were beginning to rise all around them.

Maybe it was a bad idea after all, meeting here. He should have suggested the diner on the corner. The coffee was weak, the pastry usually well on its way to stale, but at this time of the day, they would have been able to avoid prying eyes. Nothing he hated more than an invasion of privacy.

"Yes," he answered almost reluctantly.

Santini looked from one to the other, a bell belatedly going off in his head. "Then you two don't know each other?" There was audible disappointment attached to every syllable.

"Not yet," Constance replied at the same time that James uttered an emphatic, "No."

Ordinarily it was hard to hear himself think in the squad room. The constant hum of voices, computer keys clanking and phones ringing created a constant, annoying, sometimes almost overpowering din. All that had died down. All eyes were still on them, hungry now for a little action, a little amusement and diversion to momentarily make them forget about the harsh, seamy parts of life.

Annoyed by the lack of privacy, by the clear invasion he was being forced to endure, James took the woman by her arm and turned her toward his cubicle. "Why don't you come this way?"

It wasn't a suggestion. More like a command. But she wanted her mother's cameo and would have talked to the devil himself for it. Though gruff, this man didn't look as if he had a tail or cloven hooves. She figured she could easily put up with him.

Constance smiled a little wider. Mama had always told her that a woman's most effective weapon was her smile and she'd found that to be pretty accurate. Being determined and graduating at the top of her college class didn't hurt things either.

"Anything you say, Detective."

A smattering of barely concealed laughter echoed in the wake of her words, adding to James's annoyance. He brought her over to his cubicle, belatedly releasing his grip on her arm. Not for the first time, he wished he had a ceiling to go along with the walls, or at least walls that couldn't be visually breached by anyone measuring over five and a half feet.

"Have a seat." He nodded toward the chair that was butted up against the side of his desk. The chair was too close to him, but there was nothing he could do about it. He would have rather put her on the other side of the desk directly opposite him to gain more breathing room.

He watched her as she seemed to drift onto the chair rather than just sit down. She never broke eye contact, which he found a little unsettling. It seemed as if she were putting him on his guard instead of the other way around.

The best con artists had the same trait. It made them seem more trustworthy. As far as he was concerned, the woman wasn't out of the woods just yet.

Clearing his throat, he reminded himself that he was first, foremost and single-mindedly a detective. It was time he began acting like one. "Do you have any proof that the necklace—"

"Cameo," she corrected.

"Cameo," he echoed with a short nod of his head as his irritation mounted. James began again. "Do you have any proof that the 'cameo' is yours?"

"You mean like a sales receipt?" She pressed her lips together to keep from laughing. That would have been impolite.

"That would be good." The words were out before he remembered that she had said the cameo had once belonged to a family ancestor. James felt like an idiot and he was none too happy about it.

Especially when he watched the smile she was attempting to keep from her lips creeping out along her mouth anyway. "It would also be impossible. It was my great-great-great—"

"Times seven, yes, I remember now."

She was digging into her purse. For a handkerchief to dab delicately at the corners of her eyes? he wondered, a wave of cynicism getting the better of him.

But it wasn't a handkerchief. The cool Southern belle with the drop-dead legs pulled a photograph out of her purse. When she held it up for him, he saw a woman with a small girl. Though the clothes appeared somewhat out of date, he saw that the woman in the photograph was the same one sitting beside his desk. Around her neck was the cameo he'd picked up from the sidewalk.

"That your daughter?" he asked, taking the photograph from her. When she laughed, he looked up at her sharply.

"No, that's me. The little girl," she prompted when he gave her a quizzical look. "The woman wearing the cameo is my mother."

"She looks just like you," he couldn't help commenting. He handed the photograph back to her.

"She did." Unable to help herself, Constance lightly ran her fingertip along her mother's image. Time didn't help. She still missed her like crazy. "She's gone now."

That's right, he remembered. She'd said as much to him on the phone. He felt a tiny pinprick of guilt for thinking it was a ploy to get him to lower his guard. The woman at his desk looked genuinely sad as she spoke about her mother.

Uncomfortable in the face of her sorrow, James cleared his throat. "I'm sorry."

Constance inclined her head. "Everyone who ever knew her was sorry." And that had added up to a great many people. Her mother had friends everywhere. It made Constance proud.

She roused herself before the sorrow could pull her under. "And they were furious when her things were stolen." Uncle Bob had put men on it immediately. Everything was recovered within twenty-four hours—except for the cameo. It was almost as if the cameo needed to be set free for a time. There were too many strange things in the world for her to laugh away the thought when it had occurred to her. But she was glad to have the piece back. "There was a robbery at the house the day of the funeral," she explained.

He didn't believe in coincidence. Someone had to have known the house would be empty because of the funeral. "Inside job."

He looked like a man who didn't trust anyone and she wondered what had made him that way. Something drastic, she felt, her heart going out to him. He also looked like a man who would resent any charitable feelings sent his way.

"Not technically," she responded. "Turned out to be the cousin of one of the people working in the funeral parlor. He knew what time the funeral was taking place and broke in. The police apprehended him a day after the robbery."

"Fast." She heard a touch of admiration in his voice. "Was he that sloppy?"

"The police were that good," she countered. He

couldn't help wondering if she was pandering to him. "He gave everything up, including his cousin. But he didn't have the cameo. Said he didn't know what we were talking about."

He raised his eyebrow quizzically. "We?"

She flashed another smile, sending another salvo to his gut. "Sorry, I tend to lump myself in with the good guys," she continued, moving forward on the chair. Moving closer toward him, he noted. "Anyway, it's been missing for over a year and I didn't think I was ever going to get it back." She placed her hand over his, catching him completely off guard. As did the warm feeling that traveled through him, marking a path from her hand through what felt like every part of his body. "I don't know how to thank you."

Her eyes were blue. Wedgwood-blue. So blue that if he looked into them long enough, he couldn't breathe right. That's what he got for not eating lunch during his break, James upbraided himself.

"There's no need," he told her gruffly.

The man was incredibly modest. But then, she'd sensed that when she'd placed her hand on his. He was a man who preferred the shadow to the light. Preferred going his own way, unimpeded.

"Oh, but there is," she told him softly. Firmly. "That cameo has a great deal of sentimental value for me. My mother wore it when she met my father." She smiled. "As a matter of fact, that's in keeping with the legend."

His brow had knitted together in a single furrowed line. "Legend?"

"That the first time a woman puts on the cameo, she will meet her own true love within twenty-four hours."

Well, that was a load of garbage if he'd ever heard it. But the way she said it, the words sounded like gospel. She looked too intelligent to buy into something like that. And yet...

Not his business.

"That's bunk," he heard himself saying.

That he'd even use a word like *bunk* seemed out of character to him. He wondered if his sleepless nights were finally taking their toll. For the last month or so, he'd averaged less than five hours a night. Part of the problem was that he hadn't been able to shake the feeling that he was waiting for something to happen.

What, he had no idea.

She smiled at him. "Yes, I know. But the cameo still has a lot of sentimental value for me."

There didn't seem to be enough air in the cubicle. His head felt a little fuzzy. The sooner he gave her what she was here for, the sooner she'd leave. And the more air there'd be for him. "All right, then I guess a reunion is in order."

James took a key out of his pocket and unlocked his middle drawer. The cameo moved slightly as he did so, coming to rest against the center. He realized that the blue background was exactly the same shade as the woman's eyes. Come to think of it, they were the same color as the eyes of the older woman who'd discovered the thing in the first place.

He didn't like coincidences when he couldn't explain them.

He dropped the cameo into her hand, avoiding touching her skin. He didn't know why, but he just figured it was less complicated that way.

About to say something along the lines of "that being that," he found himself watching her eyes in fascination as they welled up. Damn, he hated tears. He hadn't a clue what to do when a woman cried, only that he was supposed to do something.

With a barely suppressed sigh, James looked around his desk for a box of tissues, knowing ahead of time that he wouldn't find anything.

She used the back of her hand to brush away the telltale marks. A smile returned to her lips and any tears that might have subsequently fallen held their positions.

The cameo felt warm in her hand, like something alive, connecting her to her heritage. "I didn't think I was ever going to be able to put this on."

"You've never worn it?" Thanks to Santini's neverending stories about his three girls, he was vaguely aware that daughters played dress-up with their mother's jewelry. That she hadn't seemed rather odd, given her feelings about the cameo.

Constance shook her head. "Mother was adamant about the legend. She firmly believed in it. I got engaged to Josh before she could pass the cameo on to me." She smiled as the memory came back to her. "She told me the cameo would be there waiting for me if I discovered I needed it." It was her mother's way of saying that she didn't completely approve of the match. But then, her mother wouldn't have approved of anyone that the cameo wasn't responsible for "choosing." Her mother had been very, very superstitious.

James glanced down at her left hand. He told himself that it was just an "occupational habit," taking in as much about a person as he could, to be used later. Except that in this case, there wasn't going to be a "later."

Her hand was bare.

She noticed him looking at her hand. Constance curled her fingers under her palm. "It didn't work out," she told him quietly.

Looking up at her, he shrugged dismissively. "None of my business."

An enigmatic expression played along her lips. "Wish he had felt that way. Unfortunately, he felt that everything about me was his business, especially my mother's money."

She saw the look of curiosity enter his eyes. She wondered if he was aware of it. There was no question in her mind that he was trying very hard to maintain distance between them. Asking questions, verbally or otherwise, decreased that distance.

"Josh was my mother's financial adviser," she explained, "and I discovered right after the funeral that he'd been playing fast and loose with my mother's money." Which explained the bad feeling about him that had been steadily making itself more known to her, she added silently. "Marrying me would have given him a better claim to it." Her tone became breezy, as if

she were relating just another story instead of something that had caused her a great deal of pain. "So I
broke off our engagement and I fired him."

"So now you need the cameo to help you find someone." He tried unsuccessfully to keep the touch of sarcasm out of his voice.

She raised her eyes to his. "No, I *want* the cameo
because it had been my mother's. And her mother's
before that." Her smile was warm as she added, "I
don't need a man to make me complete, Detective
Munro."

The way she said it, he believed she meant it. From
where he sat, the woman appeared to be pretty complete
as it was. He watched her untie the black velvet ribbon
and placed the cameo against her throat. She leaned her
head forward just a touch as she tied the ribbon at the
nape of her neck. Finished, she tossed her long, straight
blond hair back over her shoulder, then raised her chin
as she looked at him. Her eyes were smiling at him.
Touching him.

Which was impossible.

But he still couldn't shake the feeling.

"How does it look?" she asked.

He wasn't one to notice jewelry as a rule. But this
looked as if it belonged exactly where it was. Resting
against the hollow of her throat. Moving seductively with
every breath she took. The blue of the background made
her eyes seem even more vivid than they already were.

He was mesmerized. It took him a second to get his
bearings.

"Fine." He bit the word off, wanting to get back to something that he knew his way around.

Constance touched the cameo, as if to assure herself that it was really there. Welcome back, she thought. Her gratitude felt boundless.

"Are there some papers I need to sign?"

James shook his head. "This wasn't official police business, so no, there's nothing for you to sign." He certainly didn't require anything. "You can just go."

As quickly as possible, he added silently. Maybe if she went, the edgy feeling he was experiencing would leave with her. When she didn't rise to her feet immediately, an uneasiness undulated through him.

"I can't go without giving you some kind of reward," she protested.

There were folders all over his desk, hard copies that went along with the series of robberies he and Santini were investigating. They had yet to make it into the computer. He nodded toward them. "Letting me get back to my work is reward enough."

"No, really," Constance insisted, leaning forward. Bringing with her a whiff of something sweet and stirring. And unsettling his gut, he noted darkly.

The sooner she was gone, the sooner he could grab something to eat. "Yes, really," he insisted.

She knew ahead of time that he wouldn't accept money or a gift. He wasn't that kind of man. It didn't deter her. "There has to be something I can do. At least let me take you out to dinner."

He remained firm, fully aware that other men in his

position would have given in immediately. Having dinner with a beautiful, grateful woman, well, there were a great many worse things in life.

But one thing always seemed to lead to another, ushering in unwanted complications. Even this. It had begun as a reluctant good deed on his part and wound up turning him into the center of attention in the squad room, a position he couldn't have hated more if he tried.

The adage about no good deed going unpunished whispered through his mind.

His eyes met hers. "No need," he repeat with feeling.

Sensations rippled through her as she continued looking into his eyes. There was a need, a definite need, she thought.

Something in his eyes just beneath the surface spoke to her. Told her she was in the presence of one of the walking wounded. Her mother had always said she had a knack for finding lost spirits and restoring them.

Was that what had happened between her and Josh?

No, it wasn't, she told herself. With Josh it had been different. She'd been the one in need.

But all that was behind her.

The end result was what mattered. She hadn't made the mistake. She'd followed those unsettling instincts that had kept nagging at her, refusing to allow her to sit back and let Josh take full control of everything the way he'd kept first hinting, then suggesting, and finally insisting that he do. He'd claimed that she couldn't love him if she didn't trust him.

Truer words were never spoken.

Feeling somewhat guilty, she'd had Josh and her mother's accounts checked out by an independent third party. That had brought the truth home to her. That she's been nothing more than a walking bank account to Josh. A rather sizable bank account. Of course, it wouldn't have remained large for very long because, as it turned out, Josh Walker had lousy business instincts.

She fingered the cameo at her throat. It already felt as if she'd worn it forever. Thoughts of Josh and the mistake she ultimately hadn't made swiftly disappeared from her head.

Instead, she concentrated on the man who had reunited her with the cameo. One look at the determined set of his jaw told her that there was no arguing with the man. At least, not here. This was his terrain she was standing on.

Rising to her feet, Constance extended her hand toward him once again. His grip was firm. Like her father's used to be.

The memory warmed her.

"I really don't know how to thank you," she repeated softly.

"Then don't try."

The way he said it, she knew he thought that put an end to it. She never liked being the one owing a favor. Her mother had raised her to believe that it was far better to give than to receive—and right now, she was on the receiving end. But not for long, she promised herself as she walked out of the squad room. She nodded at Detective Santini as she passed him.

"I see it's still intact," he commented.

She looked at him curiously. "What is?"

"Your head. Munro tends to bite people's heads off—without meaning to," he explained.

She turned her head side to side for his benefit. "Yes, still there." And then she smiled at him as she left.

Santini sighed. If he didn't have a wife and three kids… Glancing toward his partner in the distance, he shook his head. Some guys had all the luck. And didn't even know it.

## Chapter Four

Stooped beneath the weight of obvious disappointment, Santini dropped into the chair that Constance had just vacated and pinned his partner with a look of utter disbelief. "And that's that?"

James shuffled through the files on his desk, trying to remember what he was supposed to do. He was in even less of a mood for what he knew was coming.

Santini rose, then sank down again. He gripped the armrests as if to provide emotional support for himself.

"You're just letting a beautiful woman—a *grateful* beautiful woman—just walk away like that?"

James spared him exactly one glance. "Couldn't think of anything to arrest her for."

Santini snorted, shaking his head. "How about possession of gorgeous body with intent to make grown men humbly drop to their knees?"

A knowing half smile lifted the corners of James's mouth as he continued his search. "Rita has you sleeping on the couch again, doesn't she?"

Santini frowned. "We're not talking about me, we're talking about you."

"No," James said with finality, closing the last uncooperative folder. "We're not." James shoved the folders into a haphazard pile. He far preferred being out in the field to dealing with paper anyway. "C'mon, let's go. We've still got that last area to canvass." He looked pointedly at his partner when the latter made no move to get up. "You know, that stuff they pay us for? It's called detective work?"

Santini looked like a man whose hot air-balloon had been shot down before it ever had a chance to begin its journey. It was clear that he was hoping to experience a little vicarious thrill. "Well, at least you know that much."

James pulled his jacket off the back of his chair, but didn't bother putting it on. The two men walked toward the doorway leading out of the squad room. "Meaning?"

Santini moved fast to keep up. "Meaning you don't know a good deal when you see one."

It wasn't a "good deal" he saw when he looked at Constance Beaulieu, it was trouble. Trouble with a capital *T*. He got enough of that on the job. "Maybe I don't want 'a good deal.'"

Santini halted just outside the squad room, looking at James as if he'd never seen him before. He lowered his voice as he asked, "Munro, you're not…?"

James gave him a dark look. "No," he said firmly, "I'm not."

"Because it's okay if you are." Santini shrugged his wide shoulders. "It's just going to take me some time to get used to, that's all."

James went to the stairwell, throwing open the fire door. He preferred taking the stairs to waiting for an elevator. It was faster. "The only thing I am is a man who's getting really close to strangling his partner. And at this point, I don't think any jury's going to convict me."

Santini followed him down. An huge sigh escaped his lips as he made it down three flights and then to the underground level behind James.

Holding the outer door open for him, James found his tolerance in short supply. "What?"

"Nothing." They made their way through the underground parking structure to where James had left the car. "Just sometimes I wonder what God was thinking, wasting all those looks on a guy who doesn't know what to do with them."

Reaching the car, James got in behind the driver's seat. The enclosed area felt stuffy. It didn't improve his mood.

"I know what to do with them." He jammed the key into the ignition and turned it. The engine hummed to life. "I wash them, I clothe them, and I get them over to a crime scene." He glanced over his shoulder to see if the way was clear. It was, but he still didn't back out. Instead, he gave Santini a warning look. "And if you don't drop this, we're going to have our own crime scene right here, right now. Except that you're not going to be in any shape to investigate. Now am I making myself clear?"

"Yeah."

Santini sounded more like a sulky child than a grade-A police detective, but he would take what he could get.

"Good. Now let's see if anyone around Playa del Rio saw or heard anything yesterday that might be useful."

For once, his partner didn't hold out much hope. "Everybody's going to have a terminal case of deafness," Santini predicted.

James slanted a final look at his partner before he pulled out of the parking structure and onto the street. "They don't know how lucky they are."

It was the usual dance. The robbers had been quick, efficient and seemed to know exactly when to strike—when the register was fullest. After questioning dozens of employees, customers and people who lived and worked in the general vicinity of all five of the restaurants that had been hit in the last five months, they were still coming up empty. There were no leads, no clues.

In the winter, that kind of thing didn't irritate him nearly as much as it did in the summer. Humidity always shrank his temper down to almost nonexistent, like a wool sweater thrown into the dryer set on hot.

The only good thing was that, confronted with the

details of the case, Santini had finally stopped yammering about the woman who had come to claim her necklace.

Cameo, he mentally corrected himself. She'd called it a cameo. Him, he didn't know the difference between a cameo and a camcorder. Things like that were Santini's department. His partner had a keen eye when it came to possessions while James had the nose for something being out of kilter. For overlooked details and things that didn't quite add up unless you tried using a different kind of math.

But not this time.

Leaving his car parked in the facility where he rented a monthly space, James crossed the street to get to his apartment. Heat rose almost like steam from the sidewalk, a testimony to the rain that had fallen earlier for a short duration. Not enough to cool, just enough to add to the stickiness of the night.

For the moment, the case had him stumped and he hated that. Hated feeling at a loss. There had to be something they were missing, some speck of a clue that by itself meant nothing but, in the proper light, made all the difference in the world.

The robberies were obviously the work of the same people. So far, though, he hadn't been able to find the connection. The restaurant employees were different at each location. No one was related to anyone else. They ordered their meats and produce from different suppliers, used different employment agencies. Nothing was the same.

Yet something *had* to be. The robberies just didn't have a random feel to them.

He tried to console himself by thinking that there would be a slipup. There always was. Someone got greedy, someone got sloppy. And when they did, he'd be there to catch them. It was as far into optimism as he ever allowed himself to venture.

Glancing at the number that registered above the elevator doors, he saw that the car was almost on the top floor. He didn't have the patience to stand here waiting for it. Muttering a curse under his breath, he took the stairs.

The back of his shirt dripped with perspiration by the time he reached the third floor. After letting himself into his apartment, James dropped his keys on the small table next to the door. He deposited his weapon in a more secure place. On top of the single bookcase that stood with its back not quite flush against the wall. The floor was uneven. Located near the subway, the apartments in the building all showed the signs of wear that came from having several trains an hour rumble by not too far from its foundations.

James stripped his damp shirt and dropped it on the recliner, which was all but buried beneath a week's worth of shirts.

He was going to have to break down and do his laundry soon, he thought. Or come to terms with smelling ripe. The idea didn't please him.

Stanley had come to life the instant James had put his key in the door. He could hear the dog's nails clicking on the hardwood floors as the animal hurried over to greet him. With a laugh, he fondly ran his hands over the dog's back. "So, how's it going, Stanley? Catch any burglars today?" The dog cocked his head and looked at him. "Yeah, me neither."

He walked over to the corner to check out the dog's water dish. There was still a little water left. He poured it out and put in a fresh supply.

The air within his apartment was a great deal cooler than outside. He'd left his air-conditioning unit on while he was gone during the day. There was no reason for both of them to suffer from the heat.

Moving over to the refrigerator, he found his every step shadowed. Stanley was shifting from foot to foot, obviously in the mood for some companionship. Dogs got bored, too, James mused. Especially intelligent ones like Stanley.

"You look better than I do," he commented. The dog barked as if in agreement. He swore that Stanley understood every word he uttered. "Tell you what, let me just recharge a little and I'll take you out on a walk. Although I warn you, once you stick your nose out there, you're going to want to come right back on the double." He fixed the German shepherd with a look. "You have to promise me, no sniff fest tonight. I've had enough heat today to last me a month."

They were outside in less than ten minutes. Despite the promise he'd tried to extract from Stanley, the dog apparently had other ideas. Every blade of weed grass that poked its head through the cracks of cement, every available place where another dog might have relieved himself, Stanley had to investigate. Not once, but twice, sniffing as if he were pulling the entire scent into his system, to file away and draw upon during those boring hours when he had the run of the apartment and the songs on the radio his master left on for him didn't interest him.

James stretched his patience to the limit. He knew that aside from the morning run, this was Stanley's only time to exercise his inquisitive mind.

But the humidity remained higher than the temperature and he was melting. It didn't exactly put him in the best of moods. After what seemed like an endless half an hour of indulgence, he turned the dog around and made his way back to his apartment.

Sometime between when they had left and returned, the elevator in his building had decided to give up the ghost. Again. That made three times in less than a month. Not a very good record, James thought darkly as he and Stanley took the stairs up to his third-floor apartment.

The stairwell seemed even more airless now than it had before, although he could have sworn there was a trace of something sweet in the atmosphere. It vaguely reminded him of the woman who'd come for her cameo.

Constance.

What a strange name, he mused.

Reaching the third floor, both master and dog paused on the other side of the fire door to draw in oxygen. Stanley was panting in Morse code and loudly at that.

"C'mon, I'll get you some water. You'll cool down," James promised, fishing through his pockets as he looked for his keys.

Had his attention not been focused so intently on his pet, he would have been alerted the second he stepped out onto the floor. There was what amounted to a one-second delay. The scent caught his attention before his eyes actually focused on the fact that there was someone standing in front of his door.

That light, honeysuckle scent that Santini had dragged into his lungs this afternoon in the same manner that Stanley took in the scent of other dogs.

The scent from the stairwell, he realized.

She was here.

Invading his space again.

He felt his spine stiffening, his body and mind on high alert. "What are you doing here?" The question was all but barked out.

She wore the same short white skirt, the same clingy light blue tank top she'd worn to the precinct. But this time, her suit jacket was slung over one arm, a casualty of the ever-increasing humidity.

He became aware that another tantalizing aroma was vying for space with her perfume, but this one had to do with food. Stanley came alive beside him the second he caught whiff of it, whimpering as if he'd been starved for the last five days.

Her eyes lit up the moment she saw him, like a Christmas tree. "Canceling out my debt."

What was with the woman—did she have some kind

of attention-deficit disorder? "I already told you, you don't owe me anything."

The expression on her heart-shaped face told him she thought differently. "Just because you think the sky's pink and say as much doesn't make it so."

He liked things plain and simple, not wrapped up in rhetoric and similes. "And what the hell is that supposed to mean?"

"That I owe you dinner—at the very least." Since he was making no move to open his apartment door, she amended her plans. She was nothing if not flexible—for the right person. "We can have it out here if you like. Like a picnic."

Whatever allure a picnic might have contained died with the boy he'd once been. He had no desire to go on one now, especially not in his own lobby. Frowning, he took the key to his apartment and opened the door.

Glancing behind him, he saw that Stanley was giving the woman the once-over, sniffing her the way he did everything new that crossed his path.

"Don't be afraid," he told her, although he had to admit, she certainly didn't look as if she were afraid. If anything, she looked as if she were enjoying the animal's attention.

Constance laughed in response. "I'm not. I love dogs." Juggling the padded carrier she was holding, she managed to pet Stanley's head.

James grunted, taking the thermal container from her. As his unwanted guest walked into the apartment, he became acutely aware of the fact that most of the clothing he owned was on rumpled display in the living room.

Putting the dark red thermal carrier down on the kitchen counter, he moved back into the living room and scooped up the pile of clothes covering one portion of the sofa, clearing off a space for her to sit, should she be so inclined. He dumped the clothes onto the recliner. They flowed over the side.

"I wasn't expecting company," he grumbled under his breath.

Constance made no effort to disguise her amusement as she glanced around. The place looked like a hurricane had gone through it—and was threatening a return match at any moment.

"Apparently." She glanced back at him. "I guess you're one of those people who likes to have everything within easy reach."

"Something like that," he mumbled under his breath. He never had anyone over, even though Santini had hinted several times for an invitation. With only Stanley for company, he had no reason to go out of his way to clean when he didn't feel like it. He didn't like being invaded and he could feel his irritation growing rapidly. "Look, how did you know where to find me?"

It wasn't as if his address was a matter of public record. He wasn't listed anywhere outside of a few official forms filed with the department, which was the way he liked it.

"I grew up calling the police chief Uncle Bob. He's not really my uncle," she explained, not wanting to mislead him, "but he was a close personal friend of my parents. I don't know what my mother would have done if he hadn't stepped in after my father died." She smiled at him as if she were talking to an old friend. "Contrary to some beliefs, not every Southern lady is actually an iron butterfly in disguise. Mama always needed someone to lean on. Uncle Bob had broad shoulders."

There was only one part of this narrative that interested him. As far as he knew, Robert Wheeler didn't come into the precinct anymore. "He's retired."

"Not from life." Besides, the man was living proof of the old saying, once a cop, always a cop. He still took an active interest in some of the larger cases, as well as fronting public relations for the department. "He still has friends in the department. I told him that you had found Mama's cameo."

She'd actually called him, asking the former chief of police if he could find out where James Munro lived since she sensed that a repeat appearance at the precinct would only embarrass James.

"He knew how much that piece meant to my mother and that I wouldn't rest until I found a way to show you how grateful I was that you took the time to put that ad in." Her eyes seemed to shine as she relayed her story. "A lot of people would have just pocketed it."

He noticed that she was still wearing the cameo. The black ribbon accented her slender neck. He found it difficult to look away. For his own safety, he figured he had better find a way. "Yeah, well, I'm not a lot of people."

"No, just one really nice man."

He was about to deny having anything to do with the word *nice* when it suddenly occurred to him that Stanley wasn't growling. The dog was his animal equivalent, taking to no one, tolerating the people around him at best—as long as they didn't invade his space.

But Stanley's space had very clearly been invaded, same as his, and instead of barking or growling, his faithful guard dog was delicately sniffing her legs and damn if the dog wasn't presenting his head to her to be petted again.

It was positively spooky. He looked at her. "You some kind of gypsy?"

She laughed. "No, just an animal lover." Forgoing, for the moment, dividing up the dinner she'd brought, Constance knelt down, unmindful of the fact that any contact with a German shepherd in the summer guaranteed her her own fur coat. "You're a handsome one, you are."

Stanley looked as if he were eating up every word. And wanted more. He curled into her hand, indicating that he wanted to be petted some more.

Still on her knees, she glanced over toward James. "I'm sorry, I forgot you had a dog, otherwise I would have brought more. But I'd be happy to share my meal with him."

James began to move over toward her to take her hand and help her up, but she effortlessly gained her feet before he could reach her. Just as well, he thought. The less physical contact, the better. Not to mention the fact that he didn't even want to know how she'd learned he had a pet.

A couple of steps had her out of the living room and in the kitchen. The clutter here wasn't any less than in the other room. There were dishes on the counter, dishes in the sink.

"Where do you keep your plates?"

He frowned, coming up behind her. "You're looking at them."

Which meant that he had no clean ones, she thought. "No problem." Before he could say anything to stop her, she was opening the cabinet beneath the sink and looking in. She found an almost empty bottle of dishwashing liquid and held it aloft like a prize. "I can just wash off three plates and we're set to go."

"Look, lady—"

The water was already running into the sink and she was squirting what was left in the detergent bottle into the steady stream.

"Constance," she corrected amiably. "Connie if you like."

What he would have liked right now was to find a way to get this woman, who was making herself more at home here than he ever had, out of his apartment.

He was also beginning to feel that the odds of that happening in the next few minutes were pretty much against him.

## *Chapter Five*

James leaned back against the counter, watching the one-woman invasion army as she quickly washed the glasses and dishes needed for the dinner she'd brought. Inexplicably, she'd made herself at home and seemed comfortable, not only within the space she had commandeered but around him as well.

Which was more than he could say. He didn't feel comfortable around her at all. But then, he had no real frame of reference to fall back on, no successful relationship to look to. His own relationship had certainly been no winner.

Growing up, he'd watched his parents argue constantly, belittling and emotionally abandoning each other at every opportunity. Try as he might, he couldn't recall a single kind word being spoken between his parents. Maybe there had been, but by then he'd done his best to shut out all the words. To shut out his parents. Silence was preferable to hoping for something better.

The one time he'd attempted to fly in the face of experience, he'd gotten badly burned. Janice, the woman he'd thought might help him limp past his emotional scars to a better place, had had baggage of her own that she'd brought to their marriage. Eventually, she'd packed it up—and their daughter Dana—and had left him. Which was only fitting because she'd left him a long time before she physically walked away.

Not that he blamed her. He was no prize. He knew that. Which was why he'd taken himself out of the storefront window and into the storeroom, resigned to making the best of what there was.

Until this woman had opened the storeroom door and begun rummaging around.

Like she was rummaging now through his cupboards.

He moved forward into the small space that comprised his galley kitchen. Stanley was right behind him, like a four-footed cheering section. He wasn't sure exactly what Stanley was cheering on.

She was standing on her toes and cocking her head to the side, trying to see into the back of his shelves. "What are you looking for?"

Constance looked over her shoulder at him, her blue eyes doing a number on his defenses. "Napkins?" She said the word hopefully, as if she wasn't quite sure if he understood what she meant.

"Don't have any." He nodded toward the paper-towel rack on the counter next to the sink. "Use those instead. Same function."

A man would think like that, she mused. "Only if you plan on being super messy." She did, however, pull two squares of paper off the roll. She found herself looking at the naked brown roll, then raising her eyes to his. "You're out of paper towels."

He met the news with a half shrug. "Not the end of the world."

"No," she agreed, "it's not. You can always use a kitchen towel in a pinch."

She looked around the cluttered counters on either side of the sink and then turned to look at the counter behind her. What she was looking for wasn't there and she'd already surveyed the inside of the cabinets.

"You don't have kitchen towels, do you?"

He chafed a little at the assumption, even though it was correct. "Are you with some national survey or the kitchen police?"

She laughed, then realized that he wasn't really making a joke; he was clearly irritated. Constance paused for a second, studying him. Most people she interacted with were friendly. If they weren't to begin with, she liked to think they became that way after a few minutes with her.

It was obvious that she was having the reverse effect on the very man she wanted to display her gratitude toward. "Are you always this touchy?"

"Only when I'm being invaded."

She turned from the sink, leaning her back against it and gazed up at him. Suddenly the small space felt smaller. It didn't help to have Stanley crowded against the back of his legs.

"This isn't an invasion, James. This is just my way of saying thank you."

He couldn't shift without calling attention to the fact that he found her closeness distracting. So he stood his ground, but not as easily as he would have liked. "A greeting card would have accomplished that."

A teasing smile began in her eyes. She turned back toward the sink, shaking off the moisture from her hands. "You would have never opened the envelope to read it." Constance looked over her shoulder as if to punctuate her statement.

His eyes met hers. He didn't like being that easily read by someone.

James swallowed a ripe curse as he reached into what was supposed to be the pantry. Boxes and jars had been thrown in there haphazardly. These items only saw the light of day when he was trying to find something. Usually unsuccessfully.

This time, though, he succeeded. The last paper towel roll from the three-pack he'd bought lay horizontally over boxes of spaghetti, jars of sauce and a myriad of not so easily identifiable purchases. Every box had some form of the word *instant* printed on it somewhere.

To James, something really wasn't "instant" unless

it jumped out of the box on its own, fully prepared and ready to consume, and sat itself down on his counter.

"Here," he growled as he pulled off the remaining plastic that clung to the fresh roll and handed the latter to Constance. "You don't have to try to drip-dry over the sink."

"Thank you," she murmured, then grinned as she delicately wiped her hands, then threw the paper towel into the garbage pail beneath the sink. "See, that wasn't hard, was it?"

"Don't push your luck, lady." He looked at the counter. Constance had set out three plates. She wasn't planning on having someone else come over, was she? "Why three?"

"One for you, one for me and one for your dog." She nodded at Stanley who was still playing her shadow. "I'm separating some of my portion for him. Ordinarily, I'd ask if you minded the dog eating off a plate, but I don't think that question really applies, here..." Her voice, echoing with amusement, trailed off as she glanced over her shoulder at the dishes that still needed to be washed. "Besides, James, you don't really strike me as the dog-food type."

Every time she said his name, it sounded like a melody on her lips. He found himself struggling to shake off the almost hypnotic effect.

"Never touch the stuff."

She laughed in response. It bothered him that he warmed to it, as if he'd performed some kind of trick for her benefit.

"I meant that I didn't see you preparing something special for your dog when you might be eating a perfectly good hamburger. You'd just share it with him."

She was right again. The woman was getting to be positively eerie.

She raised her eyes to his and knew exactly what he was thinking. She tried to put him at ease. It wouldn't do to have him spooked. Her gift made some people nervous until they got to know her.

"You've got a little ketchup on your shirt," she explained. "Dried so that I know it didn't come from anything you might have had just before you went out on your evening jog."

The explanation was for his benefit. She hadn't really analyzed it that far. She didn't have to. She had a touch of what her father's mother had liked to call "the sight." Her father's people had originally come from Louisiana and, although no one really talked about it, there had been some dabbling in the black arts by a few distant branches on the family tree.

Whether or not that had anything to do with it, she didn't know. But she'd been aware since the age of four that she'd always had a way of knowing things, sensing some things before they happened.

But her ability wasn't self-preserving. The things she knew involved other people, not herself. Which was why she'd wound up being duped by a man she'd fallen in love with. Or believed she had.

In her defense, Josh had been good. Very good at deception. And she still wanted to believe that at least a part of him had had feelings for her. But his main mistress was, and always would be, money and he'd seen a way of extending his love affair by using her. He'd swept her off her feet and would have swept her off into a marriage bed if an underlying nagging feeling that something wasn't quite right hadn't alerted her. A nagging feeling that had refused to abate until she'd finally had his dealings with her mother's funds investigated. Both before and after her mother's death.

When she'd discovered that he had been helping himself to generous portions of her mother's money, re-routing it into his own bank account for "future investment," she'd been horrified. Not to mention heartbroken. Rallying, she'd threatened Josh with legal action, knowing full well that she'd never get the money back.

He'd tried to talk her out of it, tried to undermine her determination with words of endearment, but she'd held firm. In the end, he'd cursed at her. It was the last she saw of him.

Except in her dreams.

Dreams that mocked her about her poor choice. Dreams that made her feel as if she still, despite everything, had feelings for him.

Or maybe she just didn't like the thought of being alone, she told herself.

She didn't have to be, of course. There were all those friends of her mother's to turn to if she needed anything. And her mother had left her a sizable fortune, so she was free to do whatever she wanted with her time.

She chose to work because she enjoyed it. Enjoyed being around children. Enjoyed being part of their awakening process as they opened their eyes to the world with its massive information and even greater possibilities.

"You don't have to do that, you know," James told her. "Feed him," he clarified. Stanley was once again checking her out, sniffing the bottom of her skirt. "I can just have him wait in the bedroom if he makes you uncomfortable."

"I'm not uncomfortable around your dog, James." He'd already cautioned her once about not being afraid. Did the dog have a Dr. Jekyll, Mr. Hyde kind of personality and chew on unsuspecting people? "Whatever gave you that idea? I love dogs."

Stanley had managed to weave his way between them and was now beside Constance, nudging at her legs. Checking her out and obviously liking what he discovered.

James frowned. The dog hadn't barked once at this Southern ball of fire. Had done nothing but trot after her with almost a smitten expression on his muzzle.

What the hell had gotten into his dog? It was almost as if she'd bewitched him.

"He seems to like you," he said grudgingly.

"The feeling is mutual." She addressed her words to both man and beast. Her smile, however, was meant for Stanley. "Seeing your dog just reminds me how much I miss having a pet around." She looked up at James, giving him an explanation even though he hadn't asked. "Whiskey died a little over eight months ago." She'd taken the dog's death very hard. It had come just after her breakup with Josh and it had made her feel twice as alone.

James looked at her, puzzled. "Whiskey?"

"My Labrador retriever. Her coat was the color of whiskey when the sun hits it."

"Right."

She wondered if this tall, handsome police detective possessed any imagination at all. "I'm still trying to work up my courage."

"Courage?" It was like having a conversation with a jigsaw puzzle. He braced himself, not knowing what was about to come next. "To do what?"

"To risk my heart again." She ran her hands along Stanley's coat again. If the damn dog was a cat, he would have been purring by now, James thought. "It's very hard, getting attached, knowing that things might end…"

Something in her voice caught his attention. He asked the question before he could think better of it and stop himself. "We still talking about your pet?"

Constance smiled. Maybe he did have some imagination after all. She unzipped the thermal carrier and began to divide up the food she had brought. "I can see you're a very good detective. In part."

Which meant, she was telling him, that he was half-wrong. He felt his curiosity aroused. "And in part?"

She looked down at her hand. It still felt funny looking at it and not seeing the diamond there that had rivaled the state of Texas. It had been Josh's investment in his future. One that she'd given back to him.

"I didn't come here to bore you with talk about me."

James had a feeling that it wouldn't be nearly as boring as she maintained. And it beat the hell out of delving into his life, which he sensed she was far more inclined to do.

"Well, we're not going to talk about me," he informed her.

"Fair enough. Then let's just eat."

Bending down, Constance placed the first dish she'd prepared in front of Stanley. The dog lost no time in sniffing at the offering. The investigation lasted all of one minute before he began wolfing the food down. Constance took the remaining two plates and placed them on the counter. She slid onto one of the two stools that were flush against the other side of his kitchen counter. James couldn't help noticing the way her skirt rose up on her legs as she did so.

His dog and his uninvited guest were both eating. There was nothing left for him to do but sit down on the other stool. As he did so, he looked down at the plate and, for the first time, realized that she'd brought dolmadakia, which were stuffed grape leaves, spanakopita, a kind of spinach-and-cheese pie, and keftedes, meatballs made with mincemeat, onions and bread. Greek cuisine. He was partial to Greek food, despite the fact that he had met his ex-wife in a Greek restaurant. She'd been the waitress who had taken his order.

He nudged the serving on his plate with his fork. "Dolmadakia," he murmured.

Constance raised her eyes to his, her mouth curving in a soft smile. "Yes, I know."

"Greek," he said needlessly.

Truly a man of few words, she thought as she nodded in reply. "Uh-huh."

A hint of suspicion entered his eyes. "Santini tell you I liked Greek food?"

Her expression was the soul of innocence. "The subject never came up."

It shouldn't have, and yet, here he was looking down at a plate of Greek cuisine. "Then I'm supposed to see this as some kind of cosmic coincidence?"

She slipped another piece of meat to the dog's plate. By the look on Stanley's face, James would have said that the dog had fallen in love. "If it makes you feel better to call it that, yes."

He didn't believe in coincidences. "What would you call it?"

Her mouth curved as she finished another forkful. "Delicious." The food was melting on her tongue. "Nico outdid himself."

The name meant nothing to him. He couldn't help wondering if the man attached to it meant something to her. "Nico?"

"Nico Plagianos. The man who runs the restaurant," she explained, then added, "he also runs the kitchen. He's a friend of mine."

James looked over toward the sink where she'd left the thermal carrier. The name of the restaurant was stamped across the top.

"The Greek Isles," he read out loud. The small restaurant was popular and trendy among the in-crowd. He'd heard that reservations had to be placed a month in advance. Sometimes even longer than that. As far as he knew, they didn't have takeout. Yet she had just waltzed in and gotten this order. "You know the guy who owns the Greek Isles?"

"Yes."

"And the chief of police."

She couldn't tell if he was questioning the truth of her statements, or that he was just impressed and struggling to hide the fact. "Yes."

James snorted, shaking his head. What was this woman doing here, eating with him? She was clearly out of his league. "Just what kind of a crowd do you run around with?"

"A friendly one." She placed her fork down on the plate for a moment as she looked at him. Questions stirred in her head. She'd taken in a stray once. He'd had that same wary look in his eyes as she was seeing now in James's. "And for the record, there's no running. Nico had bypass surgery last year, so he's not allowed to run and Uncle Bob's knees bother him too much to take to the track anymore." Picking up her fork, she held up the small portion she'd speared. "Good, no?"

"Yeah. Good." Excellent, actually. The food wasn't the problem. The woman who had brought it, that was the problem.

He glanced down at the floor and saw that Stanley had finished his portion and was now watching intently for anything that might have the occasion to fall off their plates.

Constance followed his line of vision and laughed. "I forgot how quick they can eat. My dog lost her appetite at the end. Broke my heart to see her turn away from everything I tried to feed her."

He knew he shouldn't ask. The more he knew, the harder it was to remain distant. But he supposed it was a harmless enough question. After all, it was just about her dog, not her. "What did she die of?"

"Being twelve. That's pretty old for a lab." A sadness twisted her lips, as if she were fighting to keep it at bay. "When she went, I felt so alone, I didn't think that I could stand it."

Despite the look on her face, he couldn't see this woman with her terminal cheerfulness succumbing to sadness. "What about 'Nico' and 'Uncle Bob'?"

She sensed he hadn't meant the question to sound sarcastic. It was his way of asking why her friends didn't fill the void. Seeing as how he had a pet himself, she figured he knew the answer to that.

"Nothing quite takes the place of a pet that loves you no matter what. Wouldn't you do anything for your dog…" She stopped, realizing that he'd never told her the animal's name. "What is his name, anyway?"

He wondered if the woman ever stopped prying. And why he kept answering her questions. "Stanley."

She pressed her lips together to keep from laughing. It struck her as an unusual name for a dog. She wouldn't have been surprised if he'd told her that the dog's name was Dog or something common, like King or Rex. Stanley, however, came under the heading of highly unusual.

"Why did you name him Stanley?"

He found himself wanting to trace her smile with the tip of his finger. The thought, the urge, came out of nowhere. He banished it back to the same region.

"I didn't," he answered curtly. "He came with that name."

He didn't go on to say that Eli had given the dog to him when the guard dog he kept at the deli had had her first litter. He didn't talk much about Eli. The subject was far too personal. And he'd already told this woman far more than he normally would have told anyone.

The sooner she left, the better.

# Chapter Six

"You don't have to do that."

They'd finished eating, but instead of taking her leave the way he thought she would, Constance had picked up their plates from the counter and slid off the stool.

She was going to wash them, he could tell by the look in her eyes. Where did she get off, making herself comfortable in his life?

To underscore his protest, James reached for the plates she was holding.

"Yes, I do."

Her voice was soft, but firm. Was her body the same way? The thought came out of nowhere, shaking him up. He didn't give a damn if she was hard, soft or in-between. He just wanted her out of here.

Sidestepping him, she went toward the sink. "If I don't, you're not going to have a single thing to eat off of tomorrow morning."

"I don't eat in the morning."

After opening the cabinet door beneath the sink, she denuded each plate of the scraps that were left. He didn't care for the way she nodded her head, as if she were privy to something about him that he wasn't. "Starting the day on an empty stomach could be why you see the world in shades of gray."

The condition of his stomach had nothing to do with the way he saw the world. He'd arrived at his view a long time ago. "There's a hell of a lot more reason for it than that."

Constance rinsed off the first dish and looked at him. "I'm willing to listen if you feel like talking."

There was compassion in her eyes and a manner about her that could have induced a clam to open and yield up its pearl. But he had decades of keeping his own counsel and he wasn't about to begin spilling his innermost feelings to a stranger—even if he could, which he didn't think was possible. You walk a certain way all of your life, you don't know how else to walk.

"Lady, the last thing in the world I want to do is talk about it."

"Maybe you'd feel better."

He'd been as polite as he was prepared to be.

"What would make me feel better is not having my space invaded."

After rinsing off the second dish, she held out her hand out for the dish that Stanley had used. It was still on the floor. "Not invading, just visiting."

"Same difference." Biting off another curse, he picked up the plate and handed it to her.

Because there was nothing else left, Constance used a little of the hand soap and applied it to the dish, rubbing it in with her fingers. Stanley had licked the plate so clean, there was nothing to remove except for the sticky residue left behind by his tongue.

She raised her eyes to James's face. "Don't know your history, do you?"

He knew as much history as the next person and didn't see where this was going. "What the hell is that supposed to mean?"

"An invasion means you stake out a place and stay for the duration, making that place yours, like a conquering army." She shook off the last dish, placing it on the rack. She was surprised he actually had one of those. "Visiting means just that, you're a tourist, passing through. Leaving."

He eyed her. "Anytime soon?"

She laughed and shook her head. If he meant to put her off, she gave no indication that he'd succeeded. "Don't exactly go out of your way to make a person feel welcomed, do you?"

Something akin to guilt pricked at him, although he wasn't altogether sure just why. After all, it wasn't as if he'd asked her to do any of this. He'd specifically tried to talk her out of it. But she had, and he supposed he could attempt to be marginally gracious about it.

James made a valiant attempt to hold on to his temper. "Look, I appreciated dinner." He waved at his dog, who was no help whatsoever. If Stanley had been true to his colors, he would have been barking at her, making her want to leave. "Stanley appreciated dinner. We probably ate better tonight than we have in a long time, but there was no need to do any of this."

She went toe-to-toe with him, although her voice was far less strained than his. "There was no need for you to put that ad in the newspaper."

He could feel his temper fraying by the moment. "I already told you. I'm a cop. It's what I do."

Her smile remained. As did she. "And I like to show my gratitude. It's what I do."

He sighed. Maybe if he waved a white flag, she'd leave him alone and go. "Consider it shown."

Well, she'd tried, she thought. And technically, she was under no obligation to take on whatever seemed to be troubling him. It was just that she hated seeing anyone in pain and whether he knew it or not, Detective James Munro was in pain.

Still, there was only so much she could do.

With a resigned sigh, she picked up her small purse. "Then I guess I'll be going."

Because he didn't trust her to actually make her way across the threshold once she reached it, James walked her. Sure enough as he opened the door for her, she turned and said, "Oh, wait."

He braced himself for anything. "Now what?"

She pointed toward the case she'd brought from the restaurant. "I forgot the thermal carrier."

The last thing he wanted to do was let her back in now that he had her so close to the door. "Hold it, I'll get it." Long strides took him to the kitchen counter and back again in a few seconds. He handed the carrier to her. "Here."

Constance felt as if she were being given the bum's rush. She wondered if that was because, in some minor way, she'd gotten to him and it made him nervous. The thought took root and she smiled to herself, knowing in her heart that she'd hit upon her answer.

What was he afraid of? she wondered. Had he been hurt like she had? Was that what made him afraid to allow another human being to come close?

Lord, she could certainly relate to that.

But she wasn't trying to get close to him in that manner. She was just trying to be a friend. And the more time she spent around him, the more she was convinced he really needed a friend. Someone to talk to who wouldn't judge him.

She paused in the doorway. "Call me if you find that you need a friend with less than four feet."

"What makes you think I don't have friends?"

Constance didn't answer. She merely smiled up at him. The knowing look in her eyes was getting to him. Irritating the hell out of him.

He blew out a breath. "Okay, thanks for dinner."

"You're welcome. Thank you for finding this." She lightly touched the cameo at her throat.

Then, before he realized what was happening, she'd risen up on her toes, brushed her lips against his cheek and was gone.

In body.

In spirit, however, she was still there, lingering on after she'd turned the corner. After he'd heard the stairwell door open and close behind her. After he'd closed and locked his own door.

It was as if she'd left a part of her essence behind. Not just the light perfume, which seemed inexplicably to expand so that it filled his apartment, but also the feel of her lips against his cheek.

Damn, but he could swear that he could still feel them on his skin, stirring up a restlessness within him he had no idea how to conquer.

He threw the second lock into place and looked down at Stanley who was staring intently at the closed door. As if willing the woman to return.

"What the hell was all that about?" he asked the dog.

Stanley had no answer.

And neither did James.


The air continued to be hot and sticky the next morning. That was the only reason he could think of why the scent of her perfume hadn't abated within his small apartment. Either that or the woman was a witch. He wasn't completely sold on the fact that she wasn't.

The previous evening and his inability to shake off its effects were responsible for putting him in a mood that caused the faint of heart to stay as clear of him as humanly possible. Nobody wanted their head handed to them.

Rather than risk losing his temper, James became quieter than usual. So much so that even Santini, accustomed to doing ninety percent of the talking, commented on the fact as they drove back from the scene of the first robbery. They'd gone there to see if they'd overlooked a possible link between the robberies.

Not finding anything added to James's overall dark mood.

Having lapsed into a two-second silence, Santini eyed his partner's chiseled, stony profile. "Trouble at the Batcave this morning?" he asked.

James gave him a look that would have sent Santini into the depths of self-imposed silence when they'd first teamed up. But Santini had learned how to roll with the punches, which was why they were still together after three years. Santini had outlasted all James's previous partners by at least two years.

When James made no answer, Santini began to play his own brand of twenty questions. "Last night?" he guessed. When James raised a brow in response, Santini figured he was on to something. "Okay, last night, then. What happened last night?"

Because bits and pieces of last night had been hovering around in his mind the better part of the day, nagging at him like a song that refused to go away, James's

response somehow slipped passed his normal tendency
to censor his own words. "She came over."

The female pronoun had Santini immediately coming to life, Pinocchio responding to a wave of the Blue
Fairy's wand.

"She? Who 'she'?" And then his eyes widened to the
size of coffee coasters. "*That* 'she'? The drop-dead gorgeous cameo 'she'?" Given James's answering glance,
Santini grinned wide enough to slip his face. "You dog,
you. You had her over."

The mention of dog made James think of Stanley.
And the betrayal he'd suffered at his pet's paws. Stanley should have barked at her, making her want to leave,
not all but lie down at her feet.

"I didn't invite her."

Santini looked baffled. "If you didn't invite her over,
how did she know where you lived?"

Pressing down on the gas, James sailed through the
yellow light before it could turn red. He had to watch himself. When he was annoyed, there was this crying need
for speed in order to vent. He had to keep it in check.

"She calls the former chief of police 'Uncle Bob.' *He*
got the address for her."

Santini took it all in like a kid listening to a bedtime
story. "Looks like you made quite an impression on her."

"No impression," James denied. "She just wanted to
show me how grateful she was."

Santini eagerly shifted in his seat, turning his body
toward James as if that would somehow make him hear
better. "And how grateful was she?"

James glanced over to see the look on Santini's face. It didn't take an FBI profiler to know what he was thinking. "Not *that* grateful. She brought dinner."

"Home-cooked?"

"Restaurant-cooked," James corrected. "From the Greek Isles."

Santini whistled, impressed. "Who did she have to kill to get dinner from there?"

"Nobody." James changed lanes. Where had all this traffic come from? This was worse than so-called rush hour, when *nothing* moved. "She knows the owner."

Santini did a quick head count. "The owner of Greek Isles, the former police chief." He nodded, pursing his lips. "Handy lady to have around."

James gave him a withering look. "I don't have her 'around.'"

"Why the hell not? C'mon, Munro, the woman's a knockout. What's wrong with you?"

Times like this, James fervently wished that the car came with an ejector seat. His or the passenger's, he didn't care which as long as one of them was gone. "I don't have time for that."

"'That' is all there is," Santini insisted. "The rest of it is what we do in order to have 'that.'" The precinct came into view. "C'mon, Munro, tell me you're seeing her again."

James gave his partner a steely look meant to shut him up. He had little hope of attaining his goal. But there was no doubt in his mind that he was definitely not going to live up to Santini's fantasy. "No, I am *not* seeing her again."

He took the long way home. His route took him by Eli's Deli. He told himself that he needed to make the stop because there was nothing edible in his refrigerator and he'd never cared for shopping in supermarkets where you needed a roadmap just to find a six-pack of beer and a loaf of bread.

But the truth of it was he wanted to see the old man's craggy face, to hear his raspy voice. Eli had seemed old to James when he'd first met him over ten years ago. He still looked the same. It was as if the man had reached a certain age and then time just stood still. That was okay by James.

Eli Levy was the reason James was who and what he was instead of some ex-convict or worse, which was the route he'd been heading on that night he'd stopped in the deli, broke and desperate.

At eighteen, he'd moved out of the house where he'd grown up because he'd been unable to remain any longer, listening to the recriminations between his parents. They had only gotten progressively heated, more venomous over the years. The acrimony had exploded like a bleeding wound when his brother, Tommy, had killed himself. Each of his parents blamed the other. He blamed them both and left. It was just as well. Word had gotten to him that they'd divorced shortly thereafter. He knew that neither one of them would have welcomed him into their house.

He bounced around, taking odd jobs, living from hand to mouth. From moment to moment. The night he walked into Eli's Deli was the lowest point of his life. With nothing in his pocket and less in his belly, he contemplated a life of crime in order to get by.

He was standing in the back of the store, seriously considering stealing the food he couldn't pay for. A strangled cry of fear at the front caught his attention and he crept up an aisle to see what was happening. A husky thug, twice as wide as he was, was brandishing a weapon, shaking it at the old woman behind the counter. Eli's wife, Sophie, he learned later. The thug was taunting her, pretending to decide who he was going to shoot first if they didn't give him the money he demanded.

At that point, angered by the gunman's audacity to threaten two old people and feeling as if he had nothing to lose, James uttered a subhuman cry and hurled himself at the gunman. He grabbed his arm, pointing it upward so that the gun discharged into the ceiling. The thug was bigger, but James had picked up a few martial-arts moves along the way. It was all he needed to use the man's size against him. He had the thug pinned down and bleeding within moments.

It was Eli who pulled James off, saying that the thug wasn't worth getting into trouble over. Sophie cried, thanking him over and over again for saving their lives even as she dialed 911.

The realization that he had actually saved them, that

he'd had the power of life and death in his hands and had chosen life, hit him with the force of a well-aimed punch to the gut. It was the first time he'd felt alive since he couldn't remember when.

After the police had come and gone and the furor had died down, Eli and his wife looked him over and came to their own conclusions. He remembered seeing a silent form of communication between the old married couple and Eli asked him if he wanted to have something to eat. Sophie, in poor health at the time, was already shuffling off to prepare what he always thought of as a feast when he looked back on it.

They invited him upstairs. They lived above the store.

And for a time, so did he.

The old couple quietly took him into their home and their hearts, encouraging him to make something of himself. For the first time in his life, he felt as if he were actually part of a family. He enrolled in a junior college, then went on to get his diploma from Queens College, getting a degree in criminology. When he graduated, Eli attended the ceremony alone because Sophie was too ill to come with him. Shortly thereafter, Sophie had died. And James had felt as if he'd lost a mother.

He looked in on Eli from time to time, worried because the man refused to sell his store and retire.

"Retire to what?" Eli would demand. "To watch my bones get old? Not me. They'll find me dead someday, still behind my counter." James knew he was serious.

When he walked in, the ancient bell that hung against

the door tinkled. A flood of memories came back to him and it took a second to shake them off.

Eli looked up from the counter. "Well, look who's here, Duchess," he called to the dog in the corner. "He looks vaguely familiar, am I right?" He pretended to scratch the few wispy white hairs on top of his head that kept him from embracing the term *bald.* "But I just can't place the name. Maybe if he came around more often, I'd remember."

James was familiar with the game. "I was here last week."

"Two weeks." Eli held up two thin fingers. "You were here two weeks ago. And three weeks before that. How slowly do you eat these days?" Eli looked him up and down, a critical expression on his face. "Too slowly, I'd say. You're getting skinny, boy." He shook his head in disapproval. "Girls don't like skinny. They like muscles." He flexed his own, which were nonexistent.

James's expression was tolerant. He loved the old man the way he never had his own father. "I'm not interested in what girls like, Eli."

Eli waved a hand at the statement, brushing it aside. "Sure you are. Don't let that one bad experience sour you on the species, boy. She had problems, that one." He seemed to note the look in James's eyes. "Okay, we won't talk about that." He spread his hands wide, to encompass the store. "What can I get you?"

The list was short. A few cold cuts, some bread and a jar of mayonnaise. It took Eli less than five minutes to prepare everything. He shook his head at the items on the counter. "You don't eat enough."

The subject of food made James think of Constance and her theory about breakfast. She would have gotten along beautifully with Eli. "I eat fine, Eli."

Eli made a face. "What? Bread and water like a prisoner?"

"Prisoners eat better than that these days, Eli," he told him patiently.

"See, even prisoners eat better than you."

In self-defense, James recited the components of his last decent meal. He should have known better. "I had keftedes, spanakopita and dolmadakia just last night."

Eli scoffed at the menu. "What, in your dreams?"

"On my plate."

Eli had been there for James when the latter had gotten divorced. Grieved with him, albeit in mutual silence, over his daughter being taken to the opposite coast. And Eli had never given up hope that someday, a woman like his Sophie would come along and win the boy's heart. Eli eyed him now. "You went out to eat?"

"No, someone brought it over." The moment the words were out, James knew he'd made a mistake.

A light no less bright than a beacon had come into Eli's eyes. "Someone? A pretty someone?"

James was about to say he hadn't noticed, but that would have been a lie. He had noticed. Which was part of the problem. He'd noticed and he didn't want to notice. More than anything, he wanted to be left alone.

Left alone to do his job, to serve and protect, eat and sleep. Nothing more.

He reached into his pocket and took out his wallet. "How much do I owe you?"

"It *was* a pretty someone," Eli cried triumphantly, ignoring the wallet held out in front of him. "Does she have a name?"

Because this was Eli and the man meant well, James held on to his patience far longer than he would have with anyone else. "Everyone has a name, Eli."

"So?" the man said expectantly, crossing his arms before him. "What's hers?"

"Constance. Constance Beaulieu."

Eli took it in, nodding his approval. "Good, solid name. She'll bear good babies."

James felt as if he'd just been broadsided by a torpedo. "Eli!"

Eli seemed unfazed by his tone. "Did Stanley like her?"

The question took James by surprise. Eli was aware of the fact that Stanley didn't take to anyone, except for him.

"Yeah. But she bribed him with food," he added quickly.

James ignored the look of triumph on the old man's face and tried again, nodding at the food on the counter. "Eli, how much do I owe you?"

"Not nearly as much as I owe you." Putting his scrawny hand over the wallet, he pushed it back toward James.

James sighed. "This is why I don't come to shop here. You won't let me pay."

Eli looked at him over the top of the rimless glasses that sat on the tip of his nose. "If I take your money, will you come more often?"

James couldn't lie, he could only do his best. "Maybe."

"That's what I thought. Put your money away. It's not any good here." Eli gave James's hand another shove for good measure, then frowned, the ruts on his face growing deeper. "Look, I need a favor."

"Anything." And he meant it. Eli was the only person in the world he would ever give his unconditional ascent to like that.

Eli beckoned him over to the rear of the counter as he spoke. There on the floor was a tall, large carton. Inside were five German shepherd puppies, all paws, floppy ears and tails.

"Duchess's last litter. I just can't seem to give these puppies away and they're beginning to eat me out of house and home. They're free, no charge," he emphasized. "Know anyone who could give one of them the kind of love they need?"

The second Eli asked, James thought of Constance.

## Chapter Seven

Looking back, James wasn't sure exactly what had come over him. Maybe it was triggered by the look he'd seen in Constance's eyes when she'd told him about losing her pet Labrador. Or maybe it was because he remembered the way she'd seemed to light up when she was petting Stanley.

Or he could just be helping Eli decrease the number of puppies he had to care for.

The last was the only excuse he felt he could deal with. Because Eli was the only person he admitted to himself that he did care about.

He watched the puppies step all over one another, trying to get his attention. Trying more to make a break for freedom. But the sides of the cardboard box were too high. There were five in all and he had to admit that they were pretty cute. Stanley had looked like that when James had taken him home. Except that Stanley had been the runt of the litter.

James shoved his hands into his back pockets to keep from picking one up. He'd leave the choice up to Eli. "I can take one off your hands."

Eli looked at him in surprise at the phrasing. "You want another dog?"

James shook his head. "No, Stanley's enough for me right now." He had no desire for more than one animal running loose in his apartment. As it was, he felt sorry for the dog being confined that way. "He'd be jealous if I brought in one of his half brothers or sisters."

"Then who's the dog for?" he asked before a light came into his gray eyes. "Hey, is this for Constance?"

James frowned slightly. "You ask too many questions, old man."

"Hey, it's not like you give up anything easily." Eli scratched the puppy under her chin. She wiggled against him in pure ecstasy. "They got action figures that talk more than you do. How am I going to know what's going on in your life if I don't ask?"

"Nothing's going on in my life, Eli." He didn't bother denying that the dog would be for Constance. Eli would just grill him until he came clean. "The woman just mentioned that she loved dogs and she'd lost hers recently. I thought that since you had extras and she had none—"

"Done." Eli joyfully declared. He transferred the puppy from his chest to James's.

James had no choice but to grab the puppy to keep her from tumbling to the floor. He looked down at the wiggly ball of fur in his arms. He shouldn't have said anything. "Doesn't have to be tonight."

"Oh yeah, it does," Eli assured him. "One less mouth to feed," he explained when James eyed him suspiciously. The old man chuckled as he watched the puppy's hind legs scrambling along James's chest, trying to get a foothold. "Wait, I'll get you a box. You don't want Felicia messing up your car."

James winced as a nail scraped against his chest. This wasn't turning out to be one of his better ideas. "You named them already?"

Eli was rummaging through possible boxes in his storeroom. "Sure I named them," he called out. "Makes things easier." After settling on a box that had the name of a popular breakfast food slapped across the sides, Eli put it on the counter, took Felicia from James and placed the puppy inside. "There. Ready to travel." His gray eyes crinkled. "Tell Constance I said hello. And bring her around sometime."

James sighed. He liked Eli, but the man firmly believed that people should go through life in pairs. Although, to his credit, Eli had been dubious about his marriage to Janice, but he'd kept his own council until Janice had split for the West Coast with Dana.

As he petted the puppy, it latched onto his finger. The

sensation of tiny little pinpricks danced all along the length of his finger. He pulled his hand away.

"You're really blowing this way out of proportion, old man."

"Hey, I can dream, can't I?" Eli patted James's hand warmly. "I want the best for you, Jimmy. And the best is a good woman. My Sophie, may she rest in peace, made my life exciting, gave me a reason to get up every morning, even when we were fighting. Because I knew if we were fighting, we'd be making up. And oh, that making up." He rolled his eyes comically heavenward.

James would have been lying if he didn't admit to envying Eli what he'd had with his wife. If it hadn't been for the couple and what he'd been privileged to witness firsthand he would have thought that all marriages were comprised of two people yelling at one another.

"They don't make women like Sophie anymore, Eli," he said quietly.

Eli inclined his head in agreement. "No, but maybe they come close. The point is, keep an open mind." James began to pick up the box with the puppy with one hand while juggling his grocery bag with the other. "Oh, wait. She'll want some dog food for her."

Moving quickly for a man approaching the midpoint of his eighth decade, Eli hurried over to the dog-food shelves and scooped up several cans. He deposited them into another bag. It was clearly more than James could manage in one trip.

"I'll walk you to your car," Eli offered.

But James shook his head. He placed the grocery bag he was holding back on the counter. "It's still ninety degrees outside. Stay here where it's cool. I'll make two trips."

Eli just gave him a withering look. "When I'm dead, you can boss me around." Taking both bags, he followed James out to his car.

It only occurred to James once he was en route. He didn't know where she lived. He made a quick pit stop home to take care of Stanley's needs, drop off his groceries and try to find Constance's address. Felicia remained in her box, which he temporarily brought into the apartment. Stanley growled his disapproval.

"Now you growl," he upbraided the dog.

It was easier to find Constance than he'd thought.

Though prepared to tap into the DMV records, Constance turned out to be listed in the first place he looked—the phone book. He would have thought someone of her background wouldn't be, would want her privacy.

But there she was, right in the middle of the page, and it didn't make sense. But then he was beginning to think that she wasn't as easy to figure out as he'd thought.

Not that he was planning on figuring her out. There was absolutely no point to that. It would be a waste of his time, seeing as how he was never going to see her again after tonight. He was just going to give her the dog and go.

End of story.

* * *

He quickly discovered the story came with an epilogue.

Constance wasn't the kind of woman you could just give something to and then leave. The trouble was, he found this out too late.

She lived in the more exclusive part of the city, in a skyscraper that came with a formidable doorman, who looked as if he'd once played linebacker with one of the pro ball teams. The man obviously would not allow James to go through without some kind of clearance from a tenant.

Without wasting time, James held up his detective's shield and tersely informed him that the puppy in the box was a surprise for Ms. Beaulieu. The harsh, lined face softened instantly. It was apparent that Constance was one of the doorman's favorites. It figured.

"She's going to love it," the big man assured him. His tone and manner implied camaraderie, as if they both cared about the woman under discussion. And that gave them some kind of bond. "She's been pretty broken up since Whiskey died. That and with her mom passing on made life pretty tough for her. That no-good fiancé of hers took a powder around that time, too."

The man peered down into the box one last time before holding a door open for an exiting tenant. Looking over the woman's head at James, he winked. "I'd say this is just what she needs."

James shifted the box. The puppy had created a dampened area on one end and he was anxious about being able to put the box down somewhere—soon. "Thanks for the vote of approval."

He realized that the doorman didn't know he was being sarcastic. Instead, the man cheerfully replied, "You're welcome. She's in the penthouse apartment," the doorman called after him as he walked into an enormous foyer.

The chandelier alone looked as if it would have set him back two years' pay—with overtime. He was definitely outclassed. James pressed for the elevator, and a sleek, mirrored car arrived almost immediately. As he stepped inside, the puppy started to whine. That made two of them, he thought, tapping the bottom of the box lightly.

Being outclassed had never bothered him before because he'd never particularly wanted to be part of any class to begin with. He told himself that things hadn't changed.

The ride to the top floor in the express elevator was quick and painless. And certainly faster his own building's elevator.

After getting off on the top floor, he didn't have to look around to find her apartment. Her apartment *was* the top floor. He rang the bell. Felicia misstepped and tumbled inside the box. He was about to ring the bell a second time when Constance opened the door.

And James came close to swallowing his tongue.

She stood in the doorway barefoot, wearing white shorts that needed an inch or two in length to qualify as cutoffs. A tight hot-pink halter top completed the outfit, if it could actually be referred to as complete. A large amount of material seemed to be missing. She made up for it in curves.

The cameo was still securely fastened around her neck. James was aware of a great deal of creamy-white skin on display.

He was also aware that he had stopped breathing for a critical amount of time. With effort, he dragged air back into his lungs before he began wheezing and embarrassed himself.

Constance was speechless.

Ordinarily, the doorbell didn't ring without the doorman first alerting her unless it was one of the neighbors dropping by. So when she opened the door to find James standing there, holding a box with a leaping German shepherd puppy, all she could do for a moment was stare.

Coming to, she looked down at the puppy, who seemed desperate to clear the sides of her confinement or die in the effort. An animal with spunk. It was love at first sight.

"May I?" she asked, indicating the puppy.

"Knock yourself out," James muttered, for the first time wishing he knew how to string more than two words together.

She laughed as the fur ball wiggled against her. A warmth sprang up everywhere the puppy touched. "Are you selling puppies door to door?"

"Yeah." Try as he might to keep a straight face, amusement curved a small portion of his mouth. "You're the last one."

He had no idea what made him say something like that. Had no idea really why he'd come or why he was still standing there like some department-store dummy. Outside of the requirements of his job, James didn't put himself out for people, had as little to do with them as possible. He was acting completely against type and that really bothered him.

"Stanley's mother had another litter," he tacked on belatedly.

Constance smiled at the news. "Sounds like Stanley's mother has a very active social life."

He shrugged the observation away. "Yeah, whatever. You said you missed having a dog and these were being given away free, so I thought…" His voice trailed off as he hoped she'd jump in and finish the sentence for him. It would have been the merciful thing to do.

"That I'd like one?" she finally guessed when James didn't go on. Her eyes lit up. All her plans about not getting attached to another animal flew right out the window. She was a sucker for a ball of fur and a pink tongue. "Yes, oh yes. I'd love one."

She held the puppy up at arm's length to get a better look at her new companion. The dog wiggled in the air, eager to get something beneath her feet again. Constance remembered James's story about Stanley.

"Does this one come with a name, too?"

"Felicia."

"Felicia," Constance repeated, then nodded her head. "I like it." Cuddling the dog against herself again, she looked at him, a different kind of warmth than before spreading through her. It was a kind thing for him to do. "Thank you."

Thanks made him uneasy, as did the look in her eyes. "Okay, then—" he started to back away, then remembered the bag of provisions at his feet. "Oh, he sent over a bag of dog food for her. In case you didn't have any," James added, feeling awkward as hell as he tripped over his own tongue.

Damn, she had him talking as if English were his second language. What the hell was going on with him, anyway? This wasn't like him. He was always in control of everything, most of all himself.

Pressing her lips together in order not to giggle as Felicia licked her ear, she tried to focus on what James was saying. "He?"

"My friend. The dog owner." Why was she asking so many questions? Why couldn't she just say thanks and close the door? It was what he would have done in her place.

"Right." That would be the man who had given him Stanley. A host of questions popped into her head, questions about his friend, about the dog. About him and why he was doing something so kind. But as James set the bag down inside the door, she saw he was already backing out again.

"You're not leaving, are you?"

He took another step back. One less step required to reach the elevator. And freedom. "Yeah, well, I've got things to see to."

She caught her lower lip between her teeth, looking

at him hopefully. "Couldn't they wait for a few minutes?"

The moment he looked into her eyes, he knew he had lost the battle.

"Okay," he relented with a sigh, "a few minutes." Picking up the bag again, he walked into the penthouse apartment. It was then that he noticed that her rugs were white. A pristine white. White rugs and puppies didn't exactly mix.

"Maybe I should have brought some carpet cleaner along," he muttered.

The sound of her soft delighted laugh passed through him like smoke through burlap. It left a mark, and he wasn't happy about that.

"They're pretty much stain resistant," she told him. "And whatever happens can be taken care of." She stroked the puppy's head with such affection that it made James's gut tighten. "It'll be well worth it."

Constance gazed at him, silently wondering about this enigma in jeans and a T-shirt. Why had he done this when good deeds clearly made him ill at ease? She had no answer, she only knew that she was glad he had.

"I don't know how to thank you, James. That's twice now you've done something wonderful for me."

He didn't want her gratitude. He didn't even know what he was doing here. Maybe there was a full moon out tonight and he was a budding werewolf. That wouldn't have been as out of character for him as bringing a puppy to a woman he barely knew. "No, I—"

Still holding the puppy to herself, she placed one finger against his lips. He felt as if he'd just been branded. "Why is it so hard for you to admit that you're a nice person, James?"

He firmly moved her hand aside, away from himself. "It's not hard. But you're blowing this out of proportion." It occurred to him that he had already uttered the exact same words this evening. To Eli. "You and Eli have a lot in common."

"Eli?" The way she said it brought up visions of cotton gins and long, languid summer nights beneath a Carolina moon.

"The owner of the dog who had the litter." There he was again, he thought in disgust, volunteering more information. For a man normally as closemouthed as he was, it was hard to accept.

He watched in fascination as she pressed her cheek against the top of the puppy's head. "I'd like to meet him sometime."

He didn't see that happening. "He owns Eli's Deli on Eighth and Fifty-third. Not exactly your neighborhood."

She glanced at him, detecting a note of superiority in his voice. People from impoverished roots wrapped themselves up in pride like that. "Do you think I'm a snob, James?"

"I think that rich girls don't go to mom-and-pop stores."

Amusement curved her mouth as she continued to stroke the puppy and hold it to herself. "Where do we 'rich girls' go?"

"Shopping," he retorted. "In fancy boutiques with overpriced things."

Rather than take offense, she merely nodded her head, taking in his words. "Have me pretty well figured out, do you?"

James shrugged in response, wishing he was in a traffic jam on the expressway. Anywhere but here, making a fool of himself for no known earthly reason.

She indicated the shorts and halter. "I bought this outfit at Old Navy the day I took my class on a field trip to show them the value of money, specifically, how to look for bargains."

He'd forgotten that she was a teacher. The fact that she taught when she could have spent days partying changed things somewhat. "They teach that kind of thing these days?"

"I don't know if 'they' do, but I do." She put the puppy down into the box for a moment. "You have to be practical. Life goes by at such a fast pace, you've got be able to jump into it with both feet and keep on running."

He wished she was still holding the dog. He felt safer with something between them. Something that would keep him from touching her the way he wanted to. "Sounds like a working-class philosophy."

"Best class there is," she said with a toss of her head. Bending over to pick up the box, giving him a very pleasant view of her hips and the way they swayed when she moved, she made her way into the living room. Her manner indicated that she wanted him to follow.

He did, never taking his eyes off her hips. His palms itched. Other parts of him grew restless. He should be heading out the door, not deeper into her lair.

She turned to face him. He had to concentrate to look into her eyes rather than at the cameo and what lay directly beneath.

Constance placed the box on the coffee table and took out the puppy again, holding it to herself. "We weren't always well off, James. My daddy got lucky when I was a little girl. But I can remember another life. My mother sitting at the table, cutting out coupons every Sunday, deciding what we could get and what we could do without until the following week. I like all this," she said, gesturing to her surroundings. "But it's not who I am."

He heard himself asking, "And who are you?"

"Just a little girl from Virginia. Oh," she laughed as the puppy began licking her face.

There was nothing little about her. Not her heart and certainly not her attributes. "Here, I'll take her," he offered, reaching for the dog. But Constance laughed and moved out of reach. She was clearly delighted with her new pet.

"I don't mind a little genuine affection, James." The dog wiggled against her, trying to use her breast for leverage in an attempt to climb up to her shoulder. For the moment, because she wanted to talk to James, she deposited Felicia back into the box. "I'm going to have to try to figure out where to let you sleep for the night." She looked at James. "I take it that she's not housebroken?"

He shook his head. "I can take her back," he offered again.

"Don't you dare," she cried, her hand immediately going toward the box protectively. "I can train her, I just wanted to know what was on my plate, that's all."

*A hell of a lot more than you probably bargained for if I don't get out of here,* he thought.

"Okay, well, I'd better be going. Stanley's waiting," he added. The second he said it, he was annoyed with himself. He never offered excuses. That wasn't his way. She was turning him inside out and yet he couldn't point to a single manipulative thing she had done. He was the one behaving strangely.

Rather than try to argue him out of it, she sensed that he needed to leave in order to collect himself. "I'll walk you to the door."

The woman hooked her arm through his as she made the offer. He brushed against her breast and felt a shaft of heat travel up his arm hot enough to singe his flesh.

"James, since you turned up again like a knight in shining armor, I was wondering if I could ask you for a big favor."

Alarms sounded in his head. He'd learned a long time ago never to agree to anything without first knowing the terms. Eli was the only exception to his rule. "Depends on what it is."

"Fair enough. I've got Career Day coming up on Friday. My speaker called just before you rang my bell and canceled on me. Airline pilot," she added. "I was wondering if you could see your way to filling in."

"I'm not an airline pilot," he pointed out dourly.

"I meant as a police detective," she clarified with a smile that got to him faster than a speeding bullet. "It would only be a ten-minute talk. Shorter if you wanted. They're just fourth graders, so it doesn't have to be anything elaborate, just something that would give them a taste of what you do. I don't think it's ever too early to introduce them to the solid choices they have before them. The more choices they have, the less likely they are to do drugs."

The sad fact of life was that there were drugs available everywhere, in both the affluent and poorer sections of the city. Suspicion nudged him. "Just where is this school?"

Constance gave him the location—not his first choice for safety. He was more than familiar with the area. "What are you doing, teaching there?"

When she looked at him, he felt something stir inside. He banked it down as she replied, "A good job, I hope."

## Chapter Eight

It took James a moment to draw his eyes away from hers and resume something that resembled clear thinking. "Look, I think you'd better find someone else to address your class."

The puppy was yipping. She scratched Felicia behind her ears. "I understand," Constance told him. "You're too busy."

She made it too easy for him.

So where was this wave of guilt coming from, threatening to drown him? He *was* busy. He and Santini were up to their armpits in restaurant robberies and clues that led nowhere, but had to be followed up nonetheless.

And yet fifteen minutes could be dug up somewhere without hurting anything.

James frowned, trying to ignore this thought. And the woman standing in front of him. He had little luck with either attempt.

"Yeah, I am busy," he told her tersely. "And besides, I don't know how to relate to kids." It was true. He felt like he'd never been a kid himself, so there was nothing to draw on there and Dana had been two when Janice, his ex-wife, had taken her away. Not that he'd done all that much interacting with the little girl up to that point, but he had always meant to. Wanted to.

Shifting Felicia around to her other side, Constance looked at him. There was an indulging expression on her face. As if she thought what he was going through was needless.

"You don't have to relate to them, James. They'll relate to you. If you just leave yourself open to the process, the kids'll take it from there," she assured him. Her smile grew, pulling him in. Taking his breath along with it. "You're an authority figure and they're at an age where they're still in awe of that, even if they don't always admit it outright."

But he shook his head, needing to stand firm. It wasn't just the kids, it was her. He had to pull back now before things got out of hand. More out of hand, he amended. He'd already gotten in further than he'd ever thought he would.

Served him right. He should have asked Santini to place the ad in the newspaper about the cameo. And he really shouldn't have come over to her apartment, bearing a dog. It gave her the wrong message. That he was interested. He wasn't interested. He wouldn't allow himself to be.

"I can't do it." His answer was firm, leaving no room for even a pin to be wedged in to widen the space for a rebuttal.

Constance was disappointed, but she did her best to cover it. Maybe it was for the best. She could feel herself being attracted to him. Her last less-than-stellar venture into the garden of romance still loomed large in her mind.

She paused to brush her cheek against the puppy's soft head. She'd always derived infinite comfort from Whiskey when she'd done that.

"All right, I can do something else that day."

For just a split second, he was jealous of a dog. He needed his head examined. She was just trying to manipulate him, he thought. Well, he wasn't buying it. "What, there's nobody else you can ask? What about the guy who cooks?"

She tried to make sense of his reference. And then she realized he was talking about Nico. "He was already there last month."

The wind left his sails. Stumped for another suggestion and wishing himself thirty stories down, in his car, he mumbled, "Well, that's not my problem."

"No," she agreed cheerfully. "It's not."

The wave of guilt grew, resembling a tsunami now. "There's nobody else you can ask?"

She moved her head slowly from side to side. "I've used everybody they might be interested in hearing."

He sighed, refusing to be taken in by the look in her eyes, the tone of her voice. He had trouble in a mono-syllabic conversation, what the hell was he going to do standing up in front of a bunch of fourth graders, deliver-ing a speech? He'd wind up tongue-tied and looking like a fool. Talking to kids was not his thing. If it had been, he would have signed up for the D.A.R.E. pro-gram a long time ago.

Enough was enough, he thought. He jerked a thumb at the doorway. "I've got to go."

Constance nodded, not offering any protest. "Thank you again. I love Felicia."

Okay, so this was a good deed, nothing more. He could live with that. Right now, he needed to get away because his knees felt funny. "I'll let Eli know."

"Thank him for me, too." She raised her voice as he took one step away. "And for the food."

"Right. Sure." All he could focus on was putting space between him and her perfume. Between him and a woman with eyes that could have been magnets. But as he attempted to turn his back on his dilemma and her, the puppy caught hold of his sleeve. Clamping down with all her might, Felicia held him fast.

"Hold it!" Constance warned, seeing the problem be-fore he was even aware of it.

He felt as if he were standing in quicksand as he swung around to glare at her. "Now what?"

"You're going to wind up tearing your sleeve," she

told him. Still holding the cloth right before Felicia's mouth to prevent any further ripping, Constance shifted the puppy back to her other arm. "I don't think Felicia wants you to go." She didn't bother looking up at him. Instead, she worked away at the material. "Wait a sec, I'll have you freed in a jiffy."

Jiffy.

Nobody said *jiffy* anymore, he thought. And nobody looked like that, either. Like they'd just stepped out of the pages of some magazine where the flattering photograph was the results of camera angles, lighting and artistic airbrushing.

Her head was bowed right before him as Constance worked the fabric out of the dog's determined teeth. He could smell her hair. Honeysuckle. Like her perfume. It filled his head, disorienting him. Making him think irrationally.

Her fingers brushed against his arm as she got the last bit of cloth out of the dog's teeth. He didn't notice the dog or the shirt. He noticed the warmth that traveled up the length of him, filling in the emptiness. Seeping into the craters that comprised the terrain of his soul.

"There," she cried triumphantly as she set the dog, now devoid of any material in her teeth, down on the floor. Her triumphant tone melted down to almost a whisper. "You're free."

They were barely an inch apart from one another. So close that their breaths mixed and became one.

All sorts of things were going on inside of him.

Things he couldn't understand or unravel. Things he felt it best not to examine.

"Not hardly," he said, more to himself than to her.

Her heart jumped up into her throat and made itself at home there just beneath the oval of the cameo.

And then everything else stopped.

For all she knew, the world had abruptly stopped turning on its axis. Because she felt the room tilting instead.

James placed the crook of his finger beneath her chin and raised her head a fraction. Placing her lips just within reach. Their eyes met and held. Seconds were knitting themselves into eternity.

She wasn't sure who cut the tiny distance between them into nothing. Probably her because, despite the fact that she was raised in an atmosphere where life was supposed to flow slowly, like warm summer breezes through cottonwood trees, there had always been an eagerness within her. An energy that wanted to reach out, seize the moment and create something out of it.

And the electricity she was feeling between them made her want to create wonderful things that touched the sky and would endure forever.

She was creating havoc, or rather, he was. Because he was kissing her. Because his hands had gone around her back and were pressing her to him now. Constance laced her fingers through his hair. She felt his body, hard, rigid and full of desire.

In less than a heartbeat, she forgot all about her promises to herself after Josh had been sent packing.

The promises that were meant to keep her away from situations just like this. To keep her safe. She needed to keep that promise because she was a lousy judge of men.

She gave her trust too easily and that wasn't safe.

Constance wasn't thinking about safe right now. She was thinking about free-falling.

And loving it.

With very little effort on his part, she could become an obsession for him. The woman he was kissing, the one he was desiring, tasted of everything precious and sweet.

And forbidden.

He had no idea what had possessed him to do this. To somehow allow himself to arrange things so that he was here, in this exact place and time, kissing her.

It only made things more difficult. He didn't want this, didn't need the added aggravation. What he needed was space. Preferably a moat between himself and the rest of the world. Specifically this woman.

*Too late.*

She probably thought he was crazy.

With a jolt, James forced himself to step away from her while everything inside of him lobbied for him to go forward. To at least kiss her longer. Until all of him was rendered totally mindless.

There were worse states to be in, that small, undermining voice whispered.

It took effort for her to catch her breath. When she could speak without a telltale wheeze, she asked, "Was that my consolation prize?"

At first, he just stared at her, not comprehending the question. "Consolation prize?"

She nodded. *Breathe, Constance, breathe.* "For not coming to speak to my class."

"No."

He was good with that word, she thought. Like an old-fashioned gunslinger who was quick on the draw, he'd whip that word out, having it explode in the air.

She nodded at his response, accepting it without argument. "It didn't feel like a consolation." She wanted to kiss him again. And she could see he wanted to leave. She wasn't going to stand in his way. "You're a hard man to figure out, Detective Munro."

He nodded, more to himself than to her. "I didn't used to be."

And with that, he left.

"You gave her a puppy?" Landing in the chair beside James's desk, Santini looked like a man who had just been struck by lightning.

"It wasn't mine," James bit off.

He wore the same jeans he'd had on last night. When he'd gone to retrieve his keys out of his pocket, he'd pulled out a dog treat. Not bothering to hide his amusement, Santini had asked him if he was carrying them around for Stanley. Which was when James had made the mistake of saying that they were for the puppy he'd brought to Constance.

He wasn't thinking clearly, but who could blame him? Every which way his mind turned, visions of last night, of kissing her and the sensations that generated through him, would take his thinking process hostage. He was completely and utterly unaccustomed to that.

Frowning now, he muttered, "Someone I know was trying to get rid of a litter and I took one off his hands. When she came over with dinner the other night, Constance said the dog she'd had died and she missed having a pet." There, that should take care of it. But it didn't. There was a smirk on Santini's face. "What?" James demanded in a barely controlled voice.

Santini attempted to look like the soul of innocence and failed miserably. The illusion of innocence had eluded him long ago.

"Nothing." He spread his hands wide, then couldn't resist adding, "Just in some countries, you'd be engaged by now."

James had no idea if he was kidding or not. Santini was a walking treasure trove of useless and near-useless information. "You've gotta make your wife let you watch something besides the Discovery Channel, Santini. You're putting my feet to sleep."

Santini eyed him knowingly. "Don't change the subject."

"There *is* no subject," he declared with a finality that was enough to jar the other man's teeth. He pushed the files they'd been going through into the middle of his desk and began flipping through them. When he'd left last night, the night-shift task force had been working on them. "Where are we on this case?"

Santini blew out a breath. "Still fishing. I know

somebody in forensic computers who's inputting all the data we've collected. She's going to try to come up with some kind of common thread besides baked goods."

"Forensic computers?" James liked to think that he kept up on the latest techniques and technology that were being brought into the department, but this was something he'd never heard of. He hated being out of the loop. "What the hell is forensic computers?"

"Just what it sounds," Santini explained.

James listened in silence. While his partner spoke, his mind was operating on a different plane, trying valiantly once more to connect the dots. Or at least to come up with a new theory about the placement of the dots.

As Santini concluded his mini-edification, something occurred to James. "Hold it. What if the common thread we're looking for is nothing we can get from the restaurant owners' input? What if the common thread is a customer?"

They'd examined employees, past and present, suppliers of every item on the menu as well as what went on the table and the linens. This was something they hadn't looked at. "Come again?"

New, with all the possibilities that entailed, the idea caught fire. "Follow me here. What if it's some guy— or woman—who frequents the place, maybe comes in at the same time every day and watches what goes on. Waiting to see when the perfect opportunity to pull off a lucrative robbery might arise."

"And just how do we find this 'common' customer?"

Santini asked. "There are no fingerprints to go on. In most cases, everything has been washed a hundred times over since the robbery took place. And most of these places don't use surveillance tapes."

"The old-fashioned way, Santini." James was already rising to his feet, ready to roll. "We talk to the waiters and waitresses to see if they noticed anyone."

"*Which* waiters and waitresses?" Santini asked.

"Which do you think?" James checked his weapon in his holster before slipping on his jacket, which felt as if it weighed a thousand pounds in this heat. "All of them."

Santini groaned, following him out of the squad room. "I was afraid you'd say that."

He hadn't lied to her.

He had too much to do. Once he'd come up with his theory of a common customer, he and Santini went at it for hours, using up that day and the next, going from one restaurant to another. They quizzed the food servers at each of the five restaurants if they'd noticed any regular customers. Each positive answer put the food server together with a police sketch artist. The sketches were compiled, then compared. It was slow going especially with the chief demanding results. There was enough work to keep them, and the night shift, busy for days.

So why was he here, standing in front of John Jay Elementary School, bracing himself to face a room full of pint-sized adults?

It didn't make any logical sense.

Neither did the way her face insisted on haunting him. In his mind's eye, he could see that look in her eyes when he'd turned her down. Over and over again. So often, part of him began to entertain the idea that he was losing his mind.

The other part was convinced he already had.

If he hadn't lost his mind, he wouldn't be down here, wouldn't have taken several hours of personal time to go to the school.

Shaking his head, he wrapped his hand around the doorknob and pulled open the door.

"All right, is everyone clear on this lesson?"

Constance scanned the room slowly. Every seat in her classroom was filled. When she had first come, she'd been warned that student "illness" was up twenty percent from the previous year. When the students did show up, the teacher often wished they hadn't. They were restless, rude and ready for trouble. Constance had set out to win over every one of them and hadn't stopped until she had. It had been tough going. Her first year had been fraught with frustration. Trust wasn't given easily, especially to someone who clearly wasn't from the neighborhood.

But she'd won her battles one student at a time. That was three years ago. Now, students came to her, begging to be allowed to take her class. The other fourth-grade teacher was now grudgingly following her lead. Constance felt each day was a mini triumph.

She glanced at the history books sitting open on the students' desks. Books she, in a good many cases because funds were short, had bought herself. She knew without asking that everyone had read the assignment. They were a good bunch of kids who wanted to learn. To make something of themselves. They had every right to expect to reach their goals, no matter how lofty. All they had to do was try. And continue to try.

A girl named Grace Mendoza raised her hand. She pointed over her head toward the door. "Ms. B., there's a man outside looking in the window. I think he's trying to get your attention."

Constance turned to look, as did the rest of her class. But they were left to speculate as to the person's identity and his reason for being there. She knew the one and hoped that she knew the other.

She tried to sound nonchalant as she said, "So there is."

Constance rose to her feet and went to open the door. Her pulse had launched itself into triple time, making all of her feel as if she were vibrating.

She glanced over her shoulder as she opened the door. "Best behavior," she instructed the class and then slipped out, closing her door behind herself.

She turned her face up to him, part of her still thinking that maybe she was just imagining all this. But then, her class would have been involved in the same hallucination. "You found the time."

She was doing it again, he thought, lighting up like a Christmas tree.

And making him want to repeat his mistake of the other night.

He deliberately kept his hands in his pockets. "Looks like. You still short a speaker?"

The look she gave him made him feel as if he were ten feet tall. "Not anymore."

"Don't expect anything good to come out of this," he warned.

"It already has," she contradicted him. He could hear the Southern lilt coming into her voice. It always seemed to appear when she spoke with emotion.

He was noticing things about her, subtle things, and that wasn't good.

Constance surprised him by taking his hand, as if he were one of her students facing stage fright. "C'mon. I'll introduce you to the class."

The noise level within the room died down the moment she opened the door. He had to admit he found that unusual. Kids were kids and noisy these days, if not worse. But then, most classes didn't have Constance as its teacher. He would have been quiet, too, if she'd been his teacher. He was more than half-convinced that she was a witch and they were under her spell. He wasn't all that sure that he wasn't, too.

"Kids, I've got a real treat for you," she announced. Letting go of his hand, she gestured toward him. "This is Detective James Munro and he's going to tell you all about what he does. I want you to give him your very best attention." Her gaze swept over them, taking in each student. "There'll be questions later."

As she indicated that he should stand in the center of the room, James thought the first question was what the hell was he doing here?

The experience turned out to be far less agonizing than he'd anticipated. He'd barely gotten started when one of the students raised a hand and asked a question. He'd no sooner answered that, than another hand shot up. And another and another. He hadn't expected questions until after he'd come to the end of his hastily composed lecture.

He discovered that it went better that way, answering questions instead of trying to figure out what to say that might interest them. The fifteen minutes she'd asked of him became twenty. And then twenty-five. Constance had to cut him short because they ran out of time. The next minute, the lunch bell rang. Everyone jumped to their feet, their minds on food and freedom.

But no one left, he noticed. They were waiting for Constance to dismiss them.

She approached the door, holding it ajar. "Okay, kids, what do you say?"

"Thank you, Detective Munro," they chorused. Constance opened the door and they filed out of the classroom. Filed, not ran, not pushed and shoved, but filed.

Once they were alone, he looked at her in amazement. "You've got them well trained."

She took no credit. "They're a good bunch of kids. They *want* to learn."

There was a huge gap between wanting to and learning. He'd found that out for himself. "That's because you make it interesting for them."

"That's all it takes," she agreed. "Interest." He could feel her eyes on him, as if she were trying to decide something. "So, how was it, talking to them? On a scale of one to ten."

He shrugged carelessly. "Five."

Constance suppressed a smile. She had a feeling that it was a little better than that, but she didn't press. He was here, which was what counted. "What made you change your mind?"

"The look in your eyes the other night before I left made me feel about ten inches tall."

That hadn't been her intent. She hated manipulation. Josh had tried to manipulate her during the course of their relationship. She'd sworn to herself that she'd never do that to anyone. "I didn't mean for it to do that."

"Yeah, you did. And it worked."

She didn't feel like arguing. Once he got to know her better, he'd realize that wasn't her way. "I'm surprised you're swayed by the look in anyone's eyes."

"That makes two of us," he replied. The words left his lips in almost slow motion.

He was keenly aware of the fact that she was standing too close again.

## Chapter Nine

It was as if his body and mind had quietly gone on automatic pilot without his knowledge.

One second, James was looking down into Constance's face, thinking that maybe he had seen more attractive women during the course of his lifetime, but even the most exceptional had not attracted him the way this woman did with her soft Southern lilt and her hypnotic blue eyes. If he listened closely, he was certain he could hear the crackle of electricity between them.

The next second, he was lowering his lips to hers without any conscious decision to do so. It just happened. Inevitably.

He *had* no say in the matter. He had to kiss her.

He had to kiss her.

Struggling for some kind of control over himself, James lightly brushed his lips against hers, silently insisting that was enough.

He rarely lied, especially to himself. He did this time. Because it wasn't enough. All it did was create a hunger in his belly for more. A hunger he couldn't deny. The look in her eyes pulled him in completely, leaving him without any kind of marker to help him find his way back.

Framing her face in his hands, his breath caught in his throat, James kissed her again. This time, there was no pretense, no attempt at a fleeting brushing of lips. This time, the kiss was more intense. Somewhere inside of him, he still hoped that he could somehow navigate his way through the rapids to the shore on the other side without being completely lost.

Hope died quickly.

In its wake came a need, a desire, the likes of which he couldn't recall ever encountering. Not even with Janice. Not even with the first woman he'd ever made love to. He knew he should be backing away. Now. While he still could. But there were forces greater than his will at work, forces that impeded his following through.

A tenth of a moment later, he forgot why he wanted to flee.

Constance knew there had to be a law on the school board books that prohibited kissing in the classroom. But until someone came and physically hit her over the head with the book that contained the rule, she was content to be blissful in her ignorance. Blissful because this man stirred up something wonderful, something delicious within her, made that much more so by the edge of danger she knew was present.

Not the danger of being discovered here with this dark, brooding detective. That was almost insignificant compared to the danger attached to caring for this man. Even now, with her head spinning out of control and her pulse rate breaking every speed record, she knew caring about James came with a penalty.

It wasn't the kind of consequence she would have had to face with Josh. Had she married Josh, she would have risked depleting her bank account.

With James, she was risking her heart.

She sensed heartbreak shimmering on the horizon. Because she had no idea if this man could ever truly open himself up the way she wanted him to.

The way she needed him to.

She had to be in touch with the person she cared about, the person she loved. The thought of continually having to knock on the closed castle door twisted her heart.

But this was logic. What she was feeling right now was light-years removed from anything logical. Light-years removed from classrooms and responsibilities.

At this moment in time, as her body leaned into his, rising in temperature, she was smack-dab in the middle of a passion that made it hard for her even to remember that breathing was a prerequisite to survival.

When he moved back, she felt herself drifting down slowly to earth, a leaf separated from the branch of the tree that had given it sustenance.

After a beat, she realized that her eyes were closed. She forced them open to look at him. Had he just gotten handsomer? More rugged? She was willing to believe anything, knowing as she did that she was on very, very dangerous ground. Crossing Niagara Falls on a tightrope made of dental floss.

She tried not to sigh and just barely succeeded. "I should have you give a talk to the students more often."

For a second, he made no response. James was struggling with an urge so basic and so adolescent he was utterly stunned by it. With the smallest of signs from her, he would have found a place, a broom closet if necessary, and made love to her until he dropped from exhaustion. Maybe then this insanity would finally drain away from him and leave him in peace.

But he was a responsible adult. A police detective for God's sake. Responsible adults didn't make love in broom closets.

Not unless there was no other choice.

But he had a choice. He had free will. Or prayed he did. Summoning it, he nodded toward the door that stood closed, a million miles away.

"I'd better be going."

She pressed her lips together, not trusting herself to

say anything coherent until she could pull all of herself together. It took longer than she'd hoped.

"Thanks for coming," she finally managed to say as she walked with him to the door.

*Out the door, all you have to do is make it out that door and you're home free,* James told himself. *Just a little farther.*

And then he stopped abruptly, knowing he was making another mistake. He turned toward her and asked, "Would you be interested in getting a cup of coffee with me somewhere? Sometime?"

Her smile went straight to his belly, curling there like smoke. "I imagine I might." Her eyes were shining again. And he was getting lost in them. Again. "Somewhere, sometime."

When his words echoed back to him, he saw how absurd they must have sounded to her. What the hell was wrong with him? This wasn't like him. He was forceful, made life-and-death decisions in a blink of an eye. How could one small-boned female change all that in less time than it took to draw breath?

"Okay." He looked directly into her eyes, challenging himself. Trying to steel himself off from her effects. "How about Friday night?"

Since she'd broken her engagement, unless there was some kind of charity function that required her presence, or a school conference taking place, Friday nights found her home with her television set and a bowl of homemade popcorn.

"Sounds perfect."

He nodded, the way he might when arranging to interview a suspect. Doing his damnedest to keep it on a less than intensely personal level. "I'll pick you up at your place. Seven-thirty."

She grinned. "Still perfect."

Her lips pursed around the second word. Temptation swooped in, whispering in his ear for him to kiss her again. But he knew if he did, he probably would opt for the broom closet.

So he mumbled goodbye and left.

Before he couldn't.

Santini combed his fingers through his wet hair, getting rid of the excess moisture. It was misting and he'd been standing on the corner for the last ten minutes, waiting for James to come by and pick him up. They were both responding to the same early-evening call that had ruined both their plans.

He'd tried several times to engage his partner in conversation. Each attempt had been met with stony silence. He'd seen Munro pensive before, but this brought new meaning to the word.

"Well, you're in one hell of a mood tonight," Santini declared, annoyed. "If you were a rain cloud, I'd be running for high ground."

They were driving down to Lexington and the scene of yet another restaurant robbery—R Squared the papers were calling it. It didn't put James in the best frame of mind. The extenuating circumstances didn't either.

He slanted a lethal glance toward Santini. "Might not be a bad idea, anyway."

But over the years, Santini had learned to stand his ground. If he didn't, Munro would plow right over him. "If I'm going to drown, mind telling me what crawled under your saddle and died?"

It was Friday night. And instead of being on his way to pick Constance up for dinner, something he'd told himself all week that he was dreading rather than looking forward to, he was driving with Santini to the scene of yet another R Squared. This time, the stakes had gotten higher. This time, someone had died at the scene.

Munro made no attempt to answer his question as he glared straight ahead at the glistening windshield with its sprinkling of summer rain.

"Hey, at least this didn't ruin your plans like it did mine." Santini's anger mounted as he talked. "Rita's mother took the kids to her house for the night. We were going to go out for dinner and a movie and then come back to an empty house." He shifted in his seat, his seat belt straining as he looked at James. "I was looking forward to getting lucky tonight."

"Lucky? You?"

Santini covered his broad chest with his hand, feigning surprise. "Hey, the sphinx speaks." He dropped his hand and his pretense. "Yeah, lucky. Don't kid yourself. It's harder for a married man with kids to get lucky than it is for a single guy." He thought of the missed opportunity and how angry Rita had been when the chief had called. They had just made it out the door when his cell phone had gone off. "Less planning went into coordinating D-Day during the World War II invasion than in arranging tonight."

James blew out a long breath. "You're not the only one who had plans tonight."

Santini's voice dripped with sarcasm. "Something good on TV tonight? C'mon, Munro, you don't date." God knew he had tried often enough to set his partner up. Rita had maybe a hundred cousins, all female. A few were sufficiently decent for James, but the latter never agreed to a setup.

When there was no answer from James, Santini's eyes widened as he stared at him. "You had a date." His voice echoed with disbelief. "With a woman?"

James debated not responding, then bit off, "Yeah, with a woman."

Feeling both relieved and incredibly let down at the same time, he had phoned Constance right after he'd received the call from the chief. She'd listened quietly, as if she'd been expecting his call all along, and then had told him that it was all right. She'd said she had papers to grade.

She'd taken the news better than he'd thought.

He wasn't sure he liked that.

Fumbling for words, he'd mumbled something about stopping by after he was done if it wasn't too late. But even as he'd said it, he knew it would be too late. Investigations didn't just neatly fold themselves up and fit into preordained slots. Depending on what they found, he and Santini could be there all night.

He realized that Santini was still talking to him.

"Who?" Santini demanded. And then, for what James saw as no earthly reason, his partner suddenly declared, "It's that woman with the cameo, isn't it?"

"Put some of those astute deductive powers to work on the case, Santini," James told him.

Technically, since he'd pulled primary on this case, he could order all the detectives assigned to the case to remain until someone found something tangible they could finally use. The robber had to get sloppy sometime. James had to concentrate to keep his mind on the case. Or cases, as it were.

As he took the corner and approached O Susannah's, where the latest robbery had taken place, he saw the usual crowd. And more. There were several cars parked in a circle, like pioneer wagons bracing for a hostile attack. But what caught his eye wasn't the ambulance or the M.E. truck. He recognized one of the cars. It belonged to another detective.

Gritting his teeth together, he said to Santini, "They've called in Homicide." Which meant interference and grappling for territorial rights. That always slowed things down considerably.

As if they were galloping along now.

He swore under his breath. It was *their* case and he and Santini were going to crack it. Without the help of any hotshot Johnny-come-latelies.

"This just keeps getting better and better," he muttered as he pulled his car up beside the M.E.'s black SUV.

It promised to be a long night. But not as long as it

was for the person inside the body bag being zipped up just as James was getting out of his vehicle.

It was after eleven and he was drained.

James knew he should just keep driving straight and head for home, drop into bed and hopefully acquire a few hours of sleep. But his brain was on overtime and he knew that sleep would elude him for hours.

Besides, he had these two large containers of coffee in his car. If he went home, they'd go to waste.

He'd found himself driving toward her part of town. Getting the coffee had been an afterthought. An excuse.

Didn't mean anything, he was just driving. The coffee was there to keep him awake. Both containers. And driving around sometimes helped work out the tension he was feeling.

Or added to it.

Looking down, he became aware that he was holding the steering wheel in a death grip with both hands. He willed himself to relax.

It took a bit of doing.

James continued driving, heading for her place even as he silently lectured himself that if he showed up on her doorstep at this hour, bearing two containers of coffee, not only might he be guilty of waking her up, but also of making her believe that there was something going on between them.

*Well, isn't there?*

It was the same annoying voice, the one that saw no

reason to give him any peace since the moment he'd first heard her voice on the telephone.

Yeah, he grudgingly admitted, he supposed there was "something" going on between them, but not *the* something. Not the kind of thing that led to long-term commitments.

As long as he kept that in mind, it would be okay to see her.

He kept on driving.

He found a parking spot less than a block away. Leaving the vehicle, he walked down the street, a container of coffee in each hand. The doorman he'd met the other day was still on duty. He greeted James with a warm look of recognition as he approached.

"Good to see you again, Detective," the man declared as he held open the door for him.

James nodded at the man.

"Here, let me get the elevator for you." For a heavy-set man, the doorman moved with surprising agility. He jabbed the button, then touched the brim of his hat. "Have a nice night, sir."

Seeing as how he was putting himself out on a skinny limb, James didn't see how a "nice night" was possible.

The ride up was even faster than he remembered, pitching his stomach against his ribs. He got off, juggling the coffee containers so that he could ring her doorbell. Mentally, he began counting. If she wasn't here by *five* he was leaving.

She was there by *three*.

The sleep that hovered around her eyes seemed to

vanish instantly the second she realized who had rung her doorbell.

"James, you did come." She threw the door open wider. "I'd given up hope."

Hoping. She'd been hoping he would come. This wasn't good. He made no move to enter, frozen there by her declaration.

"Look, if it's too late—"

"It's Friday night. That means it's not really a school night." She winked as she took his arm and coaxed him into the apartment like a newborn colt who was unsteady on his legs and wasn't quite sure what to do with them yet. "I can stay up."

The second he was inside the penthouse, he heard the sound of tiny nails pounding against the tile in a quick, staccato motion. The next moment, Felicia was there, barking, leaping and looking as if she were going to take him and his containers of coffee down.

"I think you'd better give me those." Constance laughed as she took the coffee containers.

His hands free, James stooped down and picked up the eager animal. Felicia appeared as if she were in seventh heaven, trying to lick every part of his face at once. It took effort not to laugh. The dog was a furry bundle of pure love.

He looked at Constance over Felicia's head. "How's the dog coming along?"

Constance gestured around the apartment with one container. "She has complete run of the place, so she's thrilled."

That wasn't what he meant. But a sniff of the air told him there'd been no telltale accidents. Either that, or Constance had a staff of maids who took care of that kind of thing instantly. "How's the training going?"

"Fine." She paused to grin at her pet. The dog seemed oblivious to her now that James was here. *I know where you're coming from, honey,* Constance thought. "She has me eating out of her paw."

Felicia was still licking his face a mile a minute, like a long-lost friend who had given up all hope of ever being reunited with him. The little pink tongue felt rough. He shifted the dog to his other side as he looked at Constance. "I don't exactly see you as being a pushover."

She liked the compliment. A good many people equated her soft Southern lilt to her being fairly brainless and easily manipulated. She was anything but. If she had a fault, though, it was that she was too ready to trust. To believe the best of everyone. She'd gotten a little wiser since Josh, but then, she hadn't truly been tested up to this point.

It made her a little uneasy.

"I'm afraid I am." Her eyes held his for a moment. "When it comes to a great many things. But I did manage to housebreak her before she broke the house," she added with a smile.

Walking into the spacious living room, she placed the two containers on the coffee table and sat down on the light blue sofa. The Manhattan skyline, available directly behind her thanks to the bay window, completed the picture. A complement of stars shone above her.

After a beat, he took the other end of the sofa, releasing Felicia to fend for herself. She raced around the sofa once, then sank down at his feet.

"You surprised me, showing up at this hour," Constance told him.

"Yeah, well, I guess I kind of surprised myself, too," he admitted and shrugged. "I get too wound up in a case, I can't sleep. I took a chance that you might still be up."

She held the container with both hands and drank deeply before answering. "Grading papers always takes a lot of time. Especially compositions."

"Always hated compositions," he remarked.

Her eyes crinkled into a grin. "These are about you. Career Day," she reminded him. "You made a very good impression on the class. We now have ten potential police detectives."

"Only ten?"

"Hey, it's early yet. Some of them might change their minds."

He took a long sip of his coffee, enjoying the banter. Unable to look anywhere but at her. She was wearing those white shorts again. The ones that had been produced by a manufacturer who obviously believed in economizing by husbanding his material.

He felt warm just looking at them. It was the last thing he needed. Shifting farther into his end of the sofa, he finally asked, "You got any other shorts you can wear?"

She looked down at the ones she had on. "Is there something wrong with these?"

"Yeah." He took another sip before adding, "There's not enough material."

He didn't like the way her laugh wrapped itself around him.

With a nod of her head, Constance stood up. "I see." Leaning over, she placed her container of coffee back on the table and looked as if she were about to go into the bedroom.

He was a grown man, James chided himself. He should be able to rein himself in no matter what kind of thoughts were going on in his head. Shaking his head, he stopped her before she could leave the room. "No, never mind. You don't have to change. I'll just have to deal with it."

She wondered if he realized that he'd complimented her. "You find this distracting?"

"Hell, yes."

Her grin was huge. "Good, I was hoping you would." Tucking one leg under her, she sank back down onto the sofa and reached for her coffee. James obviously needed to talk. She decided to prod him a little. "So, how's the case coming along? Or am I not supposed to ask?"

"It's an ongoing investigation."

"In other words, you're not supposed to talk about it."

He considered her carefully. "I don't figure you're going to leak anything to the press."

She pretended to zip her lips. "Anything you say here isn't going anywhere. Unless Felicia has a byline at the *Daily News* I don't know about." She cocked her head. "Might do you good to use me as a sounding board, bounce off any theories you might have." When he looked at her in surprise, she added, "Sometimes I'd stand outside the room and listen when Uncle Bob talked to Mama about a case."

Humor curved his mouth for the first time that day. "You might have gotten more than you bargained for, doing that."

She shook her head. "Wouldn't happen. Mama was completely dedicated to Daddy's memory. Which was too bad in a way. I really thought Uncle Bob would have made a great father. But the women in my mother's family are very steadfast. One-man women to the grave."

James noticed that she was fingering the cameo as she said that.

## Chapter Ten

The clock on the fireplace mantel chimed the half hour. Twelve-thirty. In the morning.

He'd stayed a lot longer than he had intended, held hostage by her soft voice, the tilt of her body as she listened intently to every syllable he uttered. Seductively pulling words out of him when he'd had no real intention of talking.

It was getting late, really late, and he had no business staying. No business being here in the first place.

Sure, he was attracted to her, but it couldn't lead anywhere. He didn't *want* it to lead anywhere. The fact that he was attracted to her, well, his parents must have been attracted to each other at one point or they wouldn't have gotten married. But they had wound up at each other's throats almost constantly and the attraction had eventually vanished.

Fighting and bitterness was all he'd seen when he was growing up. He hadn't fared much better when he'd married Janice. It wasn't the kind of thing he wanted to risk inflicting on Constance. But since he'd never experienced anything else, there was little doubt in his mind that he was capable of sustaining any positive relationship.

Which meant that he had no right to be taking up space here, space that could be used by someone else. Someone who would matter in her life.

The pinprick of jealousy unsettled him. He didn't like it. Uncertain how to deal with the emotion, he did the only thing he could. He squelched it.

"Look," he said suddenly, without preamble, "I don't know what I'm doing here."

Her smile held him in place, even as he wanted to gain his feet and leave. "Sitting. Talking. Being human." She cocked her head a little, her hair spilling down her bare shoulder. "Want me to go on?"

It was too easy to get lost in her rhetoric. In her eyes. He stayed strong. "No, you know what I mean. I don't do this kind of thing."

"Which?" she asked guilelessly. "Sitting? Talking? Or being human?"

This truth-telling was hard on him. He wasn't accustomed to explaining himself and he didn't much like it. Ordinarily, he'd just walk out. But she deserved more.

Why she deserved more was not something he was willing to delve into right now. "I don't do relationships."

She nodded, accepting his explanation. And finding a way around it. "Fine. Do one day at a time. One hour at a time. Better yet, one word at a time." She wasn't after anything beyond the moment. And helping him to connect to the world. "Not everyone has a long-range plan—"

He glanced at her and silently resisted what she was trying to do. To give him an excuse to be with her. "I do."

She raised her brow. "Oh?"

"It's to do my job and go home at the end of the day, preferably without a gunshot wound."

"And do you always want that home to be empty?"

His reply rose to his lips before he could prevent it. "It wasn't always empty." He wasn't sure what he expected or wanted to find in her eyes. Pity would have made him instantly shut down. He wasn't all that certain about his reaction to sympathy or compassion, either. "I was married once."

The revelation surprised her. Not that he had been married, but that he'd told her without being restlessly prodded. She took that as an encouraging sign that perhaps he was willing to join the real world after all. "Go on."

He didn't want to. He wanted to close the door on the subject. But he had been the one to open it in the first place, so he gave her a little more, tearing it from his soul.

"I thought I could make a go of it. I was wrong." It

hurt his pride to say that, but he told the truth. "*It* was wrong from the start."

A host of questions filled her head, but this wasn't the time to ask anything deep. "How long have you been divorced?"

"Five years." It seemed longer than that. So long that at times, it was as if that portion of his life hadn't happened at all. But it had, because he had Dana. In spirit if not in fact. "I have a daughter. Dana. She's seven, no, eight," he corrected himself. God, had it really been that long since he'd held her, barely two years old and squirming in his arms?

There was something distant in his voice. "Do you get to see her?"

He shook his head, a little surprised that he was letting Constance in this far, telling her things he didn't ordinarily talk to Santini about and the man could be relentless in his questions. "Just a couple of times a year. Janice moved to the West Coast. She says too much contact confuses Dana."

Janice. That had to be his ex-wife. "And you miss her?"

Caught up in the web of feelings the subject evoked, he didn't immediately follow her. "Janice?" It had been a while now since he even missed the idea of Janice, of a home and family. "No."

"Dana."

"Yeah. I miss her." Which surprised him because he'd never seen himself bonding with someone a generation removed. Until he'd held his daughter for the first time.

As she'd begun to grow up, she'd reminded him a

great deal of the way Tommy had been when he was her age. Open, laughing. Tommy had been sensitive. He was the one who'd suffered every time their parents had fought. As a little boy, he'd hidden in the closet, putting his hands over his ears and crying.

Unable to stand the yelling and screaming as he'd grow older, Tommy had always searched for a path to peace. He'd thought he'd found it by using drugs. Eventually they did bring him peace. Everlasting peace.

"But she's better off over there," he added before Constance could offer any sympathy. "I can't take care of a kid." An almost wistful expression passed over his face. "I hear her stepfather's a stand-up guy."

And then he stood up abruptly, blowing out a breath. Constance rose to her feet beside him. The dog, who'd dozed off at his feet, scrambled up, all paws and ears, eager to be part of whatever was happening.

James looked at Constance sternly. "Look, I told you this for a reason. I can't get involved with you."

She expected him to be direct, but this was a little too straightforward. It took her a second to collect herself. Her eyes swept over him, searching for the best way to proceed. She didn't want him against his will.

She took a deep breath, then smiled. "All right."

He'd thought she was going to argue him out of this. This approach was worse. "Stop being so agreeable. It makes me feel guilty."

She laughed, doubling up her hands. She held them up for his inspection. "I could start beating you with my fists, would that make you feel better?"

He snorted, eyeing at her hands disparagingly. "It would be a waste of energy. I wouldn't feel it."

"Don't be too sure of that, James." She lifted her chin, her eyes teasing him. "We Beaulieu women are stronger than we look."

She didn't look strong, she looked delicious. Like sin liberally spread on a cracker.

Now he was convinced that he had to be leaving.

Even so, he couldn't resist. Feathering his fingers along her throat and face, James tilted her head up just a touch more and gently kissed her.

The kiss still had the kick of a mule and went right to his gut. Each time he kissed her, it just got that much worse because it got that much more pleasurable. Reminding him just how long it had been since he'd begun his self-imposed hermitage. And just how badly he wanted to end it.

"If I don't get going now, I don't think I'll be going."

She raised her eyes to his face. She wanted to reach out, to touch his soul and help him heal. She wanted to be with him. She embraced the thought, grateful that her experience with Josh hadn't paralyzed her the way she'd feared. "Would that be so bad?"

The moment hung suspended between them.

"Yeah, it would be. For you," he added when he saw a spark of hurt entering the blue eyes. He didn't want to hurt her, he wanted to spare her.

"Thanks for the coffee," she murmured at the door. "And the conversation."

He'd spent the time talking about the facts of the various cases that had already hit the newspaper. But even that had felt somehow too intimate. Reading the phone book with her would have seemed intimate, he couldn't help thinking, given her cadence and the way Constance leaned in her body when she listened to him speak.

Her smile was teasing as she added, "Although I have to admit, you didn't give me all that much to work with. I've run into chattier squirrels during gathering season."

He noticed that she twanged a little when she said things like that, quaint sayings probably from wherever she was from. All he knew was that her voice as well as the look in her eyes pulled him in so deep, he was beginning to worry that he might not be able to come up for air.

His lips quirked into a faint smile. "Maybe I should have brought one of those squirrels along."

She inclined her head. "Next time."

There wasn't going to be a "next time," he thought. There shouldn't have been a "this time."

"Constance…"

She could see it in his eyes. He was going to say he wouldn't be coming back. Her shoulders rose and fell in a small, dismissive shrug, sending one of her straps falling from her shoulder.

For a second, it looked as if her breast was going to be exposed. James felt as if he were about to swallow his own tongue. Very gently, he eased the strap back into place.

Something hot swelled inside of her, even as she

was seized by a feeling of incredible tenderness. Some other man would have tangled his fingers in the strap and pulled it down instead. She didn't think she would have stopped him if he had. God knew there was enough sexual tension dancing between them to fill a small convention hall.

Looking back later, Constance realized that it was at this precise moment that her feelings for him began to turn serious. She wasn't a pushy person by nature. Just determined. Her mind scrambled for a way to see him again.

"There's a carnival coming up."

James felt as if he were in the middle of a meltdown. The sound of her voice dragged him back. And yet he didn't comprehend what she was saying. "What?"

"A carnival," she repeated. And it was up to her to pull it all together. "John Jay is holding its annual carnival next Saturday—"

"And you want me to come?"

"I want you to help put it together. We're looking for parents to volunteer—"

"I'm not a parent," he reminded her, then thought of Dana. "At least not to any of the kids going to that school."

She had a way around his defenses. "A policeman is a figure of authority, just like a parent. More at times."

He shook his head, a tinge of admiration filtering through him. "Do you ever take no for an answer?"

When she smiled like that, all he could think about was kissing her. This had to stop. "What's the fun in that?"

"I don't know about fun, but it's a lot less complicated." And from where he stood, simplicity was pretty damn appealing.

"No, being alone is complicated," she insisted softly. "It allows your mind to work overtime, filling your head with all sorts of things that wind up haunting you. Keeping busy is better." She was speaking from first-hand experience. "Trust me."

That was just the trouble. He didn't trust, not anymore. Perhaps not ever. He'd trusted that his heart couldn't be broken, and yet it had been. By his parents who'd been too focused on hurting each other to notice their sons. By his brother who had given up his hold on life without so much as a decent fight. And finally by Janice, whom he could have really loved if she had only helped him find his way.

Janice leaving had been the third strike in his life. He didn't have anymore time at the plate, yet here was this woman, with eyes that seemed to look right through him, pushing a bat into his hands and telling him to take another swing.

Making him want to swing again.

"Saturday," he repeated. She nodded her head, confirming the date. Because he was tempted to say yes, he shook his head. "I'm going to be busy. The case," he explained, hoping that would be the end of it.

She knew he was hiding behind his work and could understand his motives. But as afraid as she was of being hurt, she was even more afraid of never feeling again. Never experiencing the wonderful high that came from falling in love.

The high that flirted with her now.

"We'll be there in case you change your mind," she told him. "Come early if you do. We have to build all our own stands before we can set up."

For both their sakes, he knew he had to remain firm. "Sorry."

"That's okay. Drop by later then—if you can," she added, beating him to his protest. "The kids'll love to see you again."

He hardly heard what she was saying. He was too busy watching the way her mouth moved as she spoke. Unless it had to do with a case, he was a man of very little imagination. Yet, he could almost swear he could feel those same lips against his skin with each word she formed.

Damn, but he needed a vacation. A long one. It didn't matter where, he just needed to get away. But he had a feeling even that might not help. Because anywhere he went, he'd be taking himself. And it was his thoughts that were the root of his problem here.

His thoughts and Constance.

He had to get away from her. At least physically. He'd work on the other part.

"I'll see what I can do," he murmured as he left.

As he got into the elevator and watched the doors close, he congratulated himself for leaving without kissing her the way he was so sorely tempted to do.

It was a hollow triumph.

She'd been there since seven, bringing with her gallons of lemonade, soda and tons of cookies for everyone who was going to show up and share their time for a good cause. Because it was early and the school was in a rough neighborhood, Alphonso Ho, the assistant principal, a man who had gotten his college degree on a football scholarship and whose body resembled an oncoming freight train, insisted on being with her to offer his protection. This was his neighborhood. He'd been born and raised here and everyone knew not to mess with him. She thought of him as her Hawaiian guardian angel.

The children and their parents began arriving around nine. The carnival was to take place at noon. There was a lot to do and she lost no time in reorganizing everyone, seeing to it that they had the proper directions and tools to make their stands. The sound of hammering was deafening.

It was a good sound.

The cacophony of metal meeting wood was audible a couple of blocks away, which was where he was forced to park his car. He hoped it would still be there by the time he left. James wasn't naive enough to think that police plates secured his car's safety. If anything, it was probably like waving a red flag at the bad guys, but he had no choice in the matter.

As he walked onto the schoolyard, he noticed the grounds resembled a woodworking shop that had exploded. He'd never seen so much hammering before. He looked around for Constance, telling himself that if he didn't find her in the first five minutes, he was leaving. Waiting made him edgy.

There had to be at least twenty adults here and twice that number in children. He wasn't needed here.

And then he saw her.

A feeling made her look up. And see him. Sunshine sneaked out from behind the locked door and drenched everything in golden rays. She smiled at him. She had nothing else to offer.

Resigned to his fate, James crossed to her, circumventing a pair of twins who gave the impression that they'd been eating nothing but sugar for the last two weeks. They were fairly bouncing off each other.

"Hi," he called out. He noticed that a big man, his muscles bulging out from beneath his short-sleeved shirt, eyed him. Her bodyguard? he wondered. "So where do you want me?"

An answer sprang to her lips, but she thought better than to say it out loud. There were children around. And it might scare off James. God knew it was doing a number on her right now. So instead, she asked, "How are you with hammer and nails?"

"I can use one to hit the other."

"Good answer. There'll be some wood involved as well. See if you can get that worked in between."

She began leading him over to a workplace where they were going to set up the ring toss when he caught her by the arm to get her attention. She looked at him quizzically, not knowing what to expect.

"Who's the big man?"

"That's Mr. Ho. Alphonso," she said. "He's the assistant principal."

"He looks more like a bodyguard."

"That, too. He didn't think it was safe to have me come out here by myself to start setting up."

James was well acquainted with the area. The immediate schoolyard looked amazingly pristine, but less than a half a block away, graffiti littered the walls of buildings, declaring that the property belonged to the local gang no matter who paid the taxes on it.

He inclined his head toward the big man, grateful someone was looking after this woman. "He's right."

"People look out for me," she told him. "I'm safe." She picked up a folder from the lemonade table and paged through the papers until she found the directions. "Okay, I know most men shun them, but these are the directions for building the ring-toss stand."

He looked down at the pile of wood. "Is that what this is supposed to be?"

She grinned. "Can't you see it?"

"I don't have any imagination until after I've had a few beers," he told her dryly.

"I find that hard to believe."

She was standing too close again. And even though she wasn't wearing those damn shorts that were his undoing, her jeans accentuated her curves. And made his mind wander. He struggled to find something bland to discuss.

"How long has this 'annual' carnival been going on?"

There was one hammer left in the toolbox. Since Alphonso was supervising and keeping watch over them, he would have no need for it. She presented the hammer to James. "Three years."

He'd taken note of the way everyone deferred to her. She was definitely the heart of this thing. "And who came up with it in the first place?"

Taking credit for something had never seemed very important to her. "Everyone thought it was a good idea, after a while."

He wanted to pin her down. "But it was yours to begin with, wasn't it?"

Constance shrugged carelessly. "It doesn't matter who came up with it first. All that matters is if it's a good idea or not."

What kind of a person was she? He knew people who made it a point to get credit for every small thing they did. Credit was important to them.

But obviously not to Constance.

Someone called to her and she promised to be back. He allowed himself a moment to watch her walk away, then got down to business.


In no time at all, James had worked up a sweat. Given the temperature and the fact that the humidity was ten degrees higher, it didn't come as a surprise to him. His T-shirt was soaked through. Without thinking, he stripped it off and hung it from his back pocket before he picked up his hammer again.

Less than ten minutes later, Constance came by, bearing a T-shirt on her arm. She held it out to him.

"I brought you an official John Jay Elementary shirt. Extra-large, right?"

Her eyes swept over him. She tried not to let it faze

her. The man had an incredible build, which was not all that evident when he was wearing a shirt. Now she'd never be able to think of him any other way.

It would only become as soaked as the one hanging from his back pocket. "Why would I want to put that on?"

Taking the hammer from him, she pressed the shirt into his hands. "In the interest of team spirit and riot prevention."

His eyes narrowed as he accepted the shirt. "Riot prevention?"

She nodded, dead serious. "If you don't do something to cover up those rippling muscles of yours, I don't know if I can guarantee your safety much longer. I'm not sure Alphonso can, either. In case you haven't noticed—" she nodded around the schoolyard "—you're being hungrily eyed by at least a dozen mothers, not all of whom are divorced. If you don't want to risk being spirited away by a zealous mother with an overactive imagination, I strongly urge you to put this on."

He took it from her. "What about you?"

"I already have a John Jay T-shirt on," she said innocently, indicating the T-shirt that was fitting her snugly.

"No, I mean—" What was he doing, buying trouble? Fishing for a response from her? He didn't want responses. He wanted to be left alone, he reminded himself.

She placed her hand on his wrist, her eyes on his, and murmured a soft, firm reply. "If you're asking if your rippling muscles have sent my imagination into over-time, the answer is most definitely yes."

As he got back to work, he had no idea why he couldn't get the grin off his face.

## *Chapter Eleven*

When he first walked onto the school yard, James had had no intention of remaining longer than an hour. Less if possible. Though less turned out to be a word Constance was not acquainted with.

As he stood hammering together his second wooden stand, it occurred to James ever since he'd met Constance that nothing had turned out quite the way he'd thought it would.

And she wasn't his only problem. She'd brought along her own reinforcements in the form of her students. By the time she had him working on the second stand, a large number of her class had arrived. She had the students convinced that half the fun of the carnival was in helping set it up. He had more willing hands around him to help than he knew what to do with.

As far back as he could remember, he'd kept his interactions with people to a minimum, especially off the job. And especially with those who only managed to come up to a little past his belt buckle. But if he felt out of his depth surrounded by short people, none of the students gave any indication that they noticed or shared his feeling.

The next time she came around to see how things were going, she was pleased to find James hadn't surrendered his tools to another parent, hadn't called it a day and disappeared without a word to her. He was still working, supervising a little boy who was beaming as he drove a nail into a board with James guiding his small hand.

This was what she was after, getting both James and the children to a place where there was give and take. She knew the children were more than willing and it was their willingness she was counting on to guide James. Just as he was guiding Billy's hand right now.

"I see your personal assistants have mushroomed in number."

The look he gave her silently asked for rescue. "Doesn't anyone else need any help?" he tactfully suggested. He had to watch his swings in order not to accidentally bump against any of his "helpers."

She merely smiled at him and shook her head. "Not as much as you do, apparently." Her glance swept over the kids on either side of him. There were six right now, and she was willing to bet there would be more before too long. "Make sure you help Detective Munro any way you can."

A chorus of "Yes, Ms. B.," rose up from either side of him. James shot her a look that said he'd get even with her. The sound of her laugh as she walked away rippled through his belly.

It took a while, but everything was finally set up. Where a few short hours ago there had been nothing but concrete surrounding the forty-five-year-old school bound by a chain-link fence, now there were colorful stands for games and contests, things to help feed a child's imagination. Over to one side were stands covered with bright vinyl tablecloths and littered with sandwiches and desserts. Any of it could be purchased for just pennies.

James was by no means a mathematician, but it didn't take an accountant to know that if you sold something for pennies that cost dollars, you weren't exactly making a profit. It seemed to him that the real aim here was to make sure everyone had a good time and left the premises happy, and with a full stomach.

He insisted on putting five dollars into the coffee can for a ham-and-cheese sandwich whose price was set at fifty cents.

"The bread costs more than fifty cents," he commented to Constance. She produced a napkin for him as she sipped on a diet soda she'd bought from the same stand. "Donations?" James guessed, nodding toward the swiftly dwindling food supply that had been more than ample when they'd begun.

"Yes."

Something in her voice made him look at her. When he did, he had his answer. "You paid for all this, didn't you?"

Constance didn't answer immediately. Taking another sip, she smiled that same enigmatic smile she'd flashed at him earlier and replied, "Getting paid back more than I put in, James, more than I put in."

And then, because of his skeptical look, she gestured around at the school yard. There seemed to be as many students on the premises now as there were during the week. That alone seemed incredible to him. And they seemed happy to be here.

"Just look at them, James. They're having fun." He tried to focus on what she was saying and not on the fact that she threaded her arms through his as she spoke. And caused his heart rate to speed up faster now than when he was building the stands. "Not joining up gangs or getting into trouble, they're having good, clean fun," she emphasized. "Being kids. Being exactly the age they're supposed to be and not trying to impress some local tough guy so they can get into a gang."

"And what are you?" he asked, brushing aside a strand of hair from her shoulder. "Their fairy godmother?"

Her eyes seemed to shine as she considered the thought. "Hey, if the wings fit…" And then her smile slipped into something a little more serious and he knew she was speaking from the heart. "No, I'm just the one who's lucky enough to be here in order to try to help, to turn them around. Maybe to save a few of them from what they'd been raised to believe was inevitable. A destiny that would see them into an early grave." She tossed her hair over her shoulder, tossing aside the somber mood as well. "Can't think of a greater high than that."

And then, after uttering the words, she pressed her lips together, her eyes on his.

He had a feeling something was coming. He just didn't know what, or how to brace himself. He'd built everything she'd asked for, what else was there?

"Speaking of high—" He saw her eyes search his face. Was she trying to see if he was open for anything? Maybe he was at that, he thought, vaguely wondering if she'd slipped something into the sandwich's so-called secret sauce. "I was wondering if I could get you to talk to my class about the dangers of drugs."

The blow came out of the blue and he wasn't prepared for it. It brought with it a suitcase full of emotions he hadn't dealt with in a long time. Wasn't prepared to deal with now.

His voice was flat as he said, "Your school already has a D.A.R.E. program."

"Yes I know, but this would be personal for them." Her voice took on momentum, like a spring breeze shaking magnolia blossoms off the trees. "Just my class. There are a couple of boys whose older brothers—"

Finished eating, he balled up his napkin and shoved it into his pocket. "No."

He'd cut her off so sharply, so firmly, she almost felt as if she'd been physically pushed away. Rather than back off, the way she knew he expected her to, she kept her arms through his and tugged him aside until they were behind the school building.

"What did I say?" she asked him quietly.

"Your short-term memory giving you trouble?" He couldn't help the sarcasm. Right now, it was all he could do to hold himself together. Memories of Tommy, of the way he'd found his brother in the bathroom they'd shared, came vividly rushing back to him. He struggled to shut them away.

"There was a look that came into your eyes just then, like you were wounded." Because she'd seen that same look staring back at her from her mirror when her mother had finally passed away after a long illness, Constance made a guess. "Who died, James?" she asked.

His face hardened. He didn't want her prying into his life like this. She had no right to stir things up, to make him remember things. To make him feel.

"Lots of people die," he bit off coldly. "Every day."

He made her think of a dog someone had taken a stick to, a mistreated animal that trusted no one. She wasn't about to leave him in pain like that. "Who died that was close to you?"

"Why are you pushing your way into my life, Constance? Why do you have to know everything?"

"Not everything," she said simply, "just what hurts you."

He stared at her, unable to understand. His own parents had backed away from him, never taking the time to even know a single thing about him. He was nothing to the woman standing before him. Why was she so interested in him? "Are you for real?"

The smile was soft, coaxing. He felt some of his tension leaving even as he tried to make it stay, tried to use it as a barrier between them.

"The hospital that issued my birth certificate seems to think so. James, you need to talk about this, to purge whatever is tormenting you this way."

"More than you?"

"More than me," she replied, dead serious.

He blew out a breath and looked away from her. Looked back into the past. It had been, what, eleven years ago now? Damn, had that much time gone by? Where had it gone to? He couldn't remember.

"My brother," he finally said in response to her earlier question. "My brother died of a drug overdose." His mouth felt dry as a bone. "I was the one who found him. On the bathroom floor. He had a smile on his face. Like he'd finally found an answer to all his problems."

James paused, getting hold of himself. Aware that she was still holding his arm. Tethering him to this world she was trying to create. Where people were good and cared about one another. A world that didn't exist, except in her mind.

"I didn't see it coming. Maybe I didn't want to see

it coming." He shrugged carelessly. Lost. "Whatever excuse I fed myself, I didn't stop him. Didn't save him."

He sounded so alone. She wanted to hold him, to make his pain go away. "We can't save everyone," she told him softly.

He was incredulous as her words penetrated his pain. "That's funny, coming from you. You can't leave anything alone."

She lifted one slender shoulder, then let it drop. "My mother accused me once of being an overachiever. Maybe I am. I figure if I try hard enough, I'll be able to get to a few."

Which explained what she was doing as a teacher, but not what she was doing meddling in his life. Messing with his mind.

"So why are you crowding me?" he challenged. "Why aren't you just running around, saving them?" He nodded toward the school yard. "In case you haven't noticed, I'm not twelve and I'm not in any danger of joining some street gang."

"No, you're in danger of becoming part of a different kind of gang," she pointed out, undeterred. "It's the legion of the walking wounded. The walking dead."

Dead, that was the best way to describe how he felt inside. He'd been dead for a very long time. Until she'd come along and started an exhumation process.

"Look, why don't you try to save someone you can?" Her eyes never left his face. "I am."

He didn't know whether to walk away from her as fast

as he could or sweep her into his arms and kiss her, draining her of all the life-affirming essence she could spare.

He did neither. Before he could respond at all, two of her students materialized from around the corner. The taller of the two, a boy with skin as dark as a cup of hot cocoa, looked at his friend with a superior air. "See, I told you they went here."

The other boy, smaller but wider, ignored his friend. Instead, his attention was centered on James. "Can you pitch?" he asked without any preamble.

Caught off guard, James replied truthfully, "Yeah." He'd played a fair share of baseball while in high school. There was a time when he had even considered trying his hand at it professionally. Even on the third-string minors, he could have earned enough money to provide for Tommy and himself and gotten them the hell away from their parents. That had been his goal. Until that awful morning he'd found Tommy's lifeless body.

"Good. Just the guy we're looking for." Without any further elaboration, the shorter of the two boys, Justin, took him by the arm and began to lead him to a stand that offered prizes for hitting the bull's-eye three times with a softball.

James looked over his shoulder at Constance, who spread her hands wide.

"Don't look at me," she told him, a grin splitting her face, "I can't pitch to save my life."

He sincerely doubted that.

\* \* \*

For once, neither his pager nor his cell phone went off the entire day. The one time James would have welcomed the interruption, there was none. His day off remained his day off. And he was forced to remain because every time he so much as thought of leaving, another one of Constance's students would show up directly in his path with another entreaty, another question. Or just to hang in his shadow.

"I'm going to be a cop someday, too, you know. Like you. I thought I'd learn the moves now," another one of the boys told him.

"It takes more than moves," he told the boy, who looked at him with eyes that were older than they had a right to be.

"Yeah, I know."

James was convinced that Constance had set some kind of a relay system in motion, with scouts watching him for any signs of retreat.

And so, something he'd set out only to devote an hour to, if that much, wound up stretching into an all-day affair.

He wanted to mind. But he didn't.

The carnival was over by four. The school yard cleared out within a half hour after that, leaving a ghost town of empty stands as evidence of earlier activities.

James knew he should just slip away, now that the getting was good. But he found himself coming over to Constance. He had no other conclusion to draw except that he had to be a glutton for punishment. "I suppose you need help breaking all this down."

She stopped surveying the area and looked at him. She was left with five volunteers. More willing hands would be better. And if they belonged to a strong, handsome police detective who sent her pulse into double time, so much the better.

"It would be nice."

He wished she'd stop pushing him into a niche he didn't fit into. "I don't do 'nice.'" Constance cocked her head, watching him intently. By now, he'd stopped pretending he could ignore her. "What are you doing?"

"Waiting for your nose to grow—" she slid her fingertip over it "—because that's a lie and you know it. You do 'nice' very well."

He knew the futility of arguing with her. He was a quick study. "Your influence, I suppose?"

She shook her head, not about to take the credit for something he'd already possessed. "No, you did it before I met you, otherwise, you would have never placed that ad in the newspaper about my cameo." She fingered it, making sure it was still there. It was a habit she'd gotten into from the moment she'd put it on. "And then we would have never met."

"Don't make me get wistful."

She laughed. He hadn't even come close to sounding gruff. "Can't fool me, Detective Munro. I see right through that bulletproof vest of yours."

"Right, forgot you're clairvoyant." Good thing she

wasn't really a mind reader, because he could have gotten slapped for what he was thinking right now.

She was deadly serious in her protest. "Not clairvoyant, just able to see into your soul once in a while."

He decided to challenge her. In his book, clairvoyants, even beautiful ones, were just another form of fortune tellers. He didn't believe in either. "Okay, what's the view like from there now?"

Her eyes held his for a moment and, had he been superstitious, he would have said that she really was delving into his mind. "You don't want to like me, but you do."

Her words took his breath away. Because they were dead on target. He decided to push her away, once and for all. For both their good. "Lust," he corrected tersely, "the word is *lust*."

If he meant to ruffle her or send her running, he failed miserably. "That's in there, too. But not by itself."

"You don't know what you're talking about." He kept staring at her. Maybe she would respond to the truth. "Look, I've got nothing to offer. I couldn't help the three people who meant something in my life. I wouldn't admit to myself what was happening to Tommy until it was too late and as for my ex, she always said I loved my job better than I did her." The shrug was indifferent. Helpless. Just the way he felt whenever these memories returned to him. Because he could do nothing to change either of the circumstances.

"Truth is," he told Constance, saying something out loud that he had never even allowed himself to think before, "I was hiding out. I figured if I wasn't around, I couldn't screw up. But I did anyway." His expression turned deadly serious. What did it take to make this woman back off? To send her running for the hills? Or at least away from him? "Is this the kind of person you want to get mixed up with?"

She could almost feel his pain. That was the curse of being too sensitive, of being able to pick up a vibration. It wasn't just a clever nightclub routine on her part. It was true.

"You have your tenses confused, Detective. I already am 'mixed up' with you. Don't worry, James," she added quickly, "I won't ask anything of you that you can't deliver."

The look on his face was dark. "You already have."

"But you've delivered, so it doesn't really count now, does it?"

She was light, he was dark. She was hopeful, he knew the world to be devoid of hope. He was better off letting her go.

"Look, Constance—"

Whatever words he was going to offer never made it to the starting gate. Anchoring her hands on either of his shoulders, Constance rose up on her toes to press her lips against his.

The kiss unraveled his thought process to the point that he lost all sense of direction. All sense of purpose except that he needed to savor this kiss if he was going to make it to the end of the day.

Her lips felt like warm honey, pouring into his veins.

Soothing him at the same time that they somehow managed to set him on fire. It was a kiss he wanted to go on forever. But he knew it wouldn't. That made him feel too vulnerable. And he couldn't have that.

"Damn," he murmured, still holding her in his arms, "but you argue dirty."

The expression on her face told him that she had no regrets. "Best way to win. Now, if you'll excuse me, I've got a carnival to put to bed."

He looked around and saw the same volunteers she did. "Doesn't look like you have much help."

She tried to make the best of it. "People don't like signing up for the clean-up crew. There's something exciting about putting it all together and something sad about dismantling it." She raised her eyes to his and because she could sense what he was about to say, said it before him. "Kind of like a relationship, yes, I know."

"You really are clairvoyant."

She held up her thumb and forefinger, a space of an inch between them. "Just a little."

Well, clairvoyant or not, she was still just one woman and there was a lot to do here. "I suppose you'd like help."

She grinned. "You've got the sight, too." And then she turned her eyes to his, disarming him completely. "I'd love it."

As far as he knew, men and women were created with free will. His had been taken from him and placed in storage. At least as far as his dealings with her were concerned. With a sigh, he went to take apart the stand he'd built less than five hours ago.

\* \* \*

James had meant to go home once everything was dismantled and put away. Again, he was guilty of miscalculation. If his batting average had boasted these numbers in his job, he would have been back patrolling a beat or looking for work outside the field.

But then, somewhere in the back of his mind, he'd known. Known that when everything had been packed away and the school yard once more returned to its former identity, he wouldn't be going his own way. He'd be going hers.

"Where's your car parked?" He looked around but didn't see anything in the vicinity that he would have guessed belonged to her.

"In the parking garage near my apartment." He looked at her and she elaborated further. "I caught a ride here."

He scanned the yard; they were alone. "So, where is this ride of yours?"

"They went home," she said quite simply, slipping her purse strap on her shoulder.

He wasn't going to let himself get roped in immediately. He made her work for it. "How did you expect to get home?"

Her smile was pure innocence, and he found it utterly irresistible.

"I thought you might take me there."

"You were that sure I was coming? That I'd stay?"

"Let's just say I had a feeling."

"And if I got a call and had to leave?"

"But you didn't, did you?" And then, because he continued looking at her and he liked logic, she added, "There are still lots of cabs around here this time of the day."

It wasn't day, it was almost evening. Twilight was just around the corner. He frowned. "This isn't Park Avenue and you're not superwoman. Things happen to attractive women in this part of the city. Hell, they happen to downright ugly people, too."

Rather than argue the point, she commented on the part of his words he'd tossed in carelessly. "Nobody's ugly, James. Everyone's got something attractive about them."

"You really believe that?" Even as he asked, he knew that she did. It was what made her Constance.

"It's what gets me through the day."

"Anyone ever tell you that you're thinking is off?"

"No, but I suspect you might try while you're taking me home."

James sighed and began to help her pick up the tool chest she'd brought with her. He didn't like the way she had his number. No one ever had before, except Eli. James sighed. It put him at a definite disadvantage.

## Chapter Twelve

"Why don't we stop at your place first?"

The suggestion came out of the blue. For a moment, he thought he imagined it as he was pulling his car away from the curb.

James glanced at Constance before looking back on the street. The light ahead was turning red and he swore under his breath. You missed one, you missed them all. Seemed to be his luck today.

"Stop at my place? Why?"

She watched the muscle in his jaw tighten and wondered if he thought she was propositioning him. Or if he was reacting to what he presumed was just another invasion of his space. The explanation was a great deal simpler.

"Because I kept you out a lot longer than you figured and Stanley might have to go."

He'd forgotten about the dog. First time that had ever happened. He felt a sting of guilt and then remembered that he wasn't the only one in this position. "What about your dog?"

She smiled. Her puppy was well taken care of. "I knew this was going to be an all-day thing so I left Felicia with a friend. I said if it got to be too late, I'd just pick her up in the morning."

He stepped on the gas, racing to reach the intersection before the amber light went red. At this rate, the trip would take twice as long. "And he was okay with this?"

It amused her that James just assumed that her friend was a male.

"*She,*" Constance purposely emphasized, "has two little girls and they were more than okay with it. They were in heaven."

James frowned, thinking. It would be better for him if he just dropped her off at her apartment. But his place was first and although Stanley had never once had an accident since the dog had been initially housebroken, there could always be a first time. Unable to withstand an assault of mournful brown eyes, he'd been feeding the dog a lot of cold cuts lately. If Stanley got sick...

"Okay," he agreed. "I'll make a five-minute pit stop at my place."

She studied his profile. It was positively rigid. Mountains had more flexibility. She knew she was right about his feelings of invasion. "I can stay in the car if you'd be more comfortable."

Damn the woman, why was she always so accommodating? It made him feel guilty for thinking the way he did. "No, it's hot. Wouldn't want you melting all over the passenger seat."

"Thank you." When he glanced in her direction, she smiled at him as if she'd known all along it was going to turn out this way.

He muttered something under his breath and kept on driving.

Stanley was at the door, close to bolting the second they opened it.

"Guess he does have to go," James said grudgingly. The woman was right again. But the next second, the German shepherd was bestowing a sloppy greeting on Constance. She would have fallen to the floor if James hadn't reacted quickly and grabbed her. He drew his hands away the second she was steady. He nodded toward the dog. "Sorry about that."

"Never apologize for a display of genuine affection."

James felt it was safer not to reply. She had an answer for everything. Instead, he picked up the leash from the floor and held it out to the dog.

"C'mon, Stanley, let's get this over with." The dog trotted over to him and slipped his head through the loop James had formed with the leash. James glanced at her. "You can stay here until I get back."

She didn't feel like being alone just yet. All afternoon, as she'd been working, she was also struggling to keep loneliness at bay. A loneliness that periodically crept out of a dark cave and tried to capture her.

She needed help in lifting her spirits.

Constance stuck her hands into her back pockets, her expression appealing as she said, "If that's just a suggestion instead of an order, I'd like to come along."

Rocking back on her heels, she glanced around the apartment. The shambles begged for some kind of organization. If he left her here alone, she'd have to start cleaning in order to keep back her loneliness. She had a hunch he wouldn't be too happy about that.

Blowing out a breath, James recognized her offer for what it was—the best alternative. Left to her own devices, she'd undoubtedly clean his apartment and he'd probably never find anything again.

He jerked his head toward the door, silently indicating his choice. With a soft laugh, she fell into place beside him.

After riding down the elevator, they took to the street with the dog between them, the leash taut because Stanley was eager to cover every inch of ground ahead of him.

A walk. Nothing more, just a walk with a dog and a woman at dusk. It was probably one of the simplest acts in the world and yet damn if it didn't feel right to him. As if this were what had been missing from his life.

Normal.

The word shimmered before him like a heretofore unreachable prize. There had been a time when he would have given anything to have an average, normal life, but that hope had faded along with his childhood.

And now, out of the blue, here was a woman whom he would have called anything but average, creating the illusion for him.

It was an illusion, wasn't it?

He didn't know.

"So, what did you do today, Stanley?" she asked the dog just before they came to the corner.

The animal looked over his shoulder at her, as if contemplating an answer.

The Walk sign lit up and they hurried across. "You're one of those people who thinks dogs understand us when they talk to them, aren't you?"

The way he said it, it sounded almost like an accusation. Didn't he believe in anything?

"They do understand us. It's like with a baby. If you talk to them enough, they wind up learning the language." And then she smiled knowingly. "I don't suppose that was ever your problem, talking a lot."

He didn't like the way she just took things for granted about him. He especially didn't like the fact that she was right. "You always butt into people's lives and start rearranging things?"

Stanley pulled them to a small clump of green shoots arranged in a tiny area where a square of concrete had been removed. She hurried to keep up. "Never really thought about it. That could be your problem, you know. You overthink things."

The look he gave her couldn't be defined as friendly. "My only problem, as I see it, stands about five-four and has blond hair."

Very slowly, Constance shook her head from side to side, her eyes never leaving his. "That's not your problem."

Standing back while Stanley investigated previous visitors to the small square, James watched her. Behind Constance, the moon was beginning to take its place in the sky, casting probing silver fingers through the gathering night. He tried not to notice that there were things going on inside of him, reactions occurring that shouldn't be. But were.

A lot she knew, he thought.

The moment James walked across the threshold into his apartment, he knew.

Knew he wasn't driving her home tonight.

He couldn't struggle any longer against this need that had been his steady, tormenting companion since he'd first kissed her. He wasn't going to bed, to lie awake wanting her.

Not tonight.

Tonight he'd stop being strong, stop pretending he was a man of iron and allow himself to be made of flesh and blood. Turning, he looked into her eyes and saw that she knew it, too.

Holding his breath, telling himself he was insane, he reached behind her and closed the door. The movement brought him close to her. So close he could feel her breath on his chest. Could taste her desire.

Or was that just his engulfing them both?

Everything felt tangled up, especially him.

He moistened his dry lips, searching for his resolve. His control. He went on searching. "I should take you home."

There was no conviction behind his words.

She was afraid to breathe, afraid that what was shimmering before her would be pulled away, like some prize on an invisible string. "You are home," she told him quietly.

"You know what I mean."

"Maybe better than you," she murmured.

He didn't doubt it. She seemed to be one step ahead of him all the time.

"You're in my head." It was both an accusation and a description. Because she'd been in his head almost constantly of late. Appearing before him like some kind of mirage. Making him ache. Driving him crazy. Just how much was a man supposed to take and still continue living his life?

Hope flared all through her. Constance glanced up into his eyes. "Am I, James? Am I really?"

"Yeah." His tone wasn't friendly. He was fighting for his life. "And I wish you'd get out."

*Let me in, James. Let me in.* She didn't move back. She hardly took a breath. Afraid of chasing away the moment. Chasing away the promise. "I'm not responsible for what you're thinking."

He didn't know about that. "Yes, you are. You're some kind of witch, a beautiful blond, Southern witch who's cast some kind of spell over me. And I don't like it," he insisted. He felt as if he were fighting for his sanity. "I don't like thinking about you all the time." He decided to tell her exactly what was on his mind. Hoping it would scare her away. Because God knew he didn't have the strength to push her away. "Wondering what it would be like to have you, to peel those clothes off you a little at a time and run my hands over your body."

She could almost feel them on her and the excitement that generated heated her body. "Hands-on experience is always the best," she counseled, her voice low, husky, shredding the last of his self-control so that he had nothing to hold on to.

He tried one last time to save himself. And her. He nodded toward the door. "I won't stop you if you wanted to leave."

She didn't even look. The door was a million miles away. "I'm not leaving."

Unable to hold back any longer, he took her into his arms, his body heating to a temperature he was certain would incinerate him within a few moments. Putting him out of his agony.

"Then this is on your head."

Her heart already hammered wildly beneath the thin cotton tank top. Like James, she was afraid of what was ahead of them, of her. But she recognized it as a good fear. A fear that made her risk herself. A fear that told her if all went well, there would be a reward far greater than she'd anticipated.

"Yes," she told him, "it is."

Maybe she didn't understand, hadn't understood him earlier when he'd told her that he had nothing to offer her. That three of the four people who had ever mattered to him were either dead, or disillusioned and gone.

"Constance—"

She didn't want to talk anymore. Constance pressed her body against his. "James, if you don't kiss me now, I swear I'm going to explode."

It was exactly the way he felt.

"Can't have that."

Without another word, James brought his mouth down to hers.

Until he did, he hadn't realized the full extent of just how much he'd wanted to kiss her. Everything came together in that single moment in time. Almost as if he became another person. Someone lighter, someone happy even.

His mouth slanted over hers again and again, each time James lost himself a little more. And found himself renewed. He could feel his need for her, his need to make love with her, coursing through his veins. Hardening his body. Desire sent a rhythm pulsing through him that only seemed to increase.

Finding the snap at the top of her jeans, just below her belly button, he flicked it apart with his thumb and forefinger. For the time being, he resisted the temptation to slip his hand between the thicker material and her underwear. To touch her tantalizing skin.

Instead, he slid her jeans down her taut, slender hips. He felt her wiggle ever so slightly between his palms, sending his pulse soaring.

The scrap of material she wore was a thong, and this

information registered in the distant recesses of his brain, setting the rest of him on fire. James pressed her against himself, absorbing her heat into his body, feeling weak and powerful at the same time.

He was afraid that if he gave in to the appetites churning inside of him, he would hurt her. Yet he wanted to go fast in order to satisfy this huge, gnawing hunger that ravaged him. But he knew that would frighten her. It damn well scared the hell out of him. He was just barely able to hang on to his own courage as he pushed forward.

When she placed his hands on either side of her hips and guided them down along her body, taking her thong down along with them, he thought he was pretty damn sure he was going to swallow his own tongue.

The next moment, breathing hard, Constance was stripping away his T-shirt. Her long, cool fingers slid along his belly as she worked the snap open on his jeans.

It came undone. Her eyes met his, but he couldn't read them. His gut tightened as she urgently tugged away the denim material from his hips and down his thighs. He kicked his jeans aside. His briefs followed.

The next moment, molding her against himself, they both tumbled onto his sofa.

She was still wearing her tank top and bra and it was all he could do not to tear them off her. Steadying his hands as best he could, he pulled off one, unclasped the other.

And then she was naked.

As naked as he was. As naked as the desire that beat wildly in his chest.

He kissed her again, hard, as if his very life hung in the balance. All the while his hands roamed over her, touching her, exploring her. He brought his mouth down to kiss every newly freed inch of her. Like a man who had been on a hunger strike and had suddenly been locked in a restaurant overnight, he wanted to be everywhere at once, sampling everything.

He wanted to have her and still hold off. It wasn't easy.

The latter, he knew, would provide more pleasure for her, so he did his best to rein himself in. Because it wasn't just about him. This was about her. About Constance. She had brought him to this place with her mouth that was so quick to laugh and her eyes that saw right through him. Right into him.

To her, lovemaking had never been just about passion, it was a way of giving comfort as well. She wanted to comfort James, to bring him a measure of peace. But what she wanted and what was happening were two very different things. She didn't have the upper hand here, wasn't in control of her own responses. She couldn't think clearly, couldn't see beyond the heat of the moment.

Rather than easing the sadness in his eyes, Constance found herself scrambling as one wave of pleasure crescendoed, bringing another, even higher one in its wake. They burst within her body, taking her prisoner, making her weak. Making her want more.

Anticipation steepled, stealing away the very air in her lungs.

He was creating one climax after another within her, making her vibrate like a tuning fork. They were as varied as snowflakes, no two alike. She had to catch herself before she started to sob his name.

This was supposed to be about him; how had it turned around to be about her? About drenching her in pleasures, making her forget herself. Making her crave.

Twisting and turning beneath his hand, beneath his wondrous lips and tongue, she arched hard as his mouth suckled her breast. Just as she didn't think she could take any more, he forged a moist trail along her ribs, her belly, down to the very heated core of her.

She lost track of time, lost track of everything but the fiery excitement he had created and sustained within her. Breathing hard, Constance desperately tried to pull air into her lungs. He'd stolen it from her, stolen everything but the deep, intense joy radiating to all parts of her.

Her fingers kneading his back, she watched his face as she opened for him, conveying a silent invitation. She needed to be one with him. To seal herself to him with a silent promise.

None of the shots were his. She'd called them all, like a siren. He was powerless against her and had come to hear her song. It echoed within his head.

"You are a witch," he rasped hoarsely and then he drove himself into her.

Sheathed, an urgency seized him and he began to

move to a tempo that was beyond him to change. The rhythm increased and they raced for the summit together. She arched higher, he pushed harder and heard her cry out his name against his ear a second before the supreme pleasure rocked them.

Something squeezed his heart. Hard. Holding on to her tightly, he prayed that the feeling would last even as he knew it couldn't. Even as he wondered what had come over him even to believe that it might.

The euphoria was gentle, holding him in its grasp longer than he thought possible. And then slowly, he came back to earth. And the darkness that was waiting to swallow him up again.

With it came regret.

Pivoting on his elbows, he looked down at her. "Look, I'm—"

She pressed her finger to his lips.

"Shh. Don't apologize. Don't explain. Don't talk." She wrapped her legs around him, as if to hold him within her a moment longer. To keep them one a moment longer. "Some things don't need words."

Sanity reclaimed him. What the hell had he allowed to happen? "We can't—"

"We did." Her eyes glinted.

"But we shouldn't have," he told her flatly. "I shouldn't have."

Was it so terrible, making love with her? Or was there something else tormenting his soul? Was he as afraid of risking his heart as she was? The moment she wondered, she knew.

"You're overthinking again," she told him softly. "Just enjoy it. You're allowed to feel pleasure, James. Allowed to feel happy, even if it's just for a second. Really."

There she went with that soft, Southern lilt, arguing for possession of his soul. Somehow managing to fish it out of the black hole where it had gone to take up its residence.

He could feel himself wanting her again.

Cupping the back of her head with his hand, he drew her up to him, his eyes making love to her a moment before he brushed his lips against hers.

"Now you're learning," she whispered against his lips just before she allowed herself to sink into the kiss. Back into his arms.

This time, the lovemaking went slower. This time, the frantic urgency wove itself into a tapestry that settled on his shoulders, cloaking them both.

When she matched him movement for movement, exploration for exploration, he felt he had crossed over into a new frontier. The lovemaking between them had taken on a balance he'd never experienced before. He wasn't merely making love to her, merely pleasuring her, she was making love to him. Pleasuring him. Creating a balanced union.

It would have scared the hell out of him had he been able to realize what was going on. But his mind had taken a hiatus, temporarily abdicating and allowing sensations to take over.

They did with a passion.

## Chapter Thirteen

The sound penetrated his brain slowly.

The ringing noise pulled apart the mists in his mind. By the third ring, James knew his life was calling him, putting an end to the fantasy he'd allowed himself to pretend was real.

Swallowing a resigned sigh, he sat up.

"That's yours," Constance told him in case he was wondering. "Mine plays 'Dixie.'"

He couldn't help smiling. Of course, he thought. Getting off the sofa, it took him a moment to find his jeans and the cell phone that was still in his pocket. "Munro."

He was magnificently, unselfconsciously, naked. A

feeling of intimacy seeped through Constance that had nothing to do with lovemaking and everything to do with loving. She was just going to have to find a way to deal with that, in case she was in this by herself.

Constance watched as his shoulders grew rigid. Work, she thought. Probably his partner calling. Very quietly, she slipped off the sofa and began to gather together her things. By the time James turned around, snapping the cell phone shut, she was dressed.

His eyes met hers. "I have to go."

"Yes, I know." And then because he was probably wondering if she'd had some kind of premonition, she explained. "Intuition."

Having pulled on his underwear, he reached for his jeans again, hurrying into them. "I'll drop you off," he told her.

Lifting a pile of laundry, she looked around for her purse. His apartment really could stand a cleaning. But volunteering would send him the wrong signals. And undoubtedly send him running for the hills.

"I can get a cab if you're in a hurry."

"I'll drop you off," he repeated more firmly.

"Fine." To show her compliance, she paused and lightly brushed a kiss against his lips. She caught him completely unprepared. "I never argue with the long arm of the law."

He didn't believe that for a single moment. "You'd argue with God and probably have a fifty-fifty chance of winning."

As he walked out of the apartment with Constance just ahead of him, he noticed that she didn't bother to dispute his words.

Santini was already on the scene when James arrived. The latest restaurant to be hit was located downtown. His hair only a little less rumpled than his clothing, James's partner came over to him with the stats on the latest robbery.

The last of the sleepy look left Santini's eyes as he paused and smiled at him. "Sorry to have to drag you away from her."

James glanced at him sharply. "What the hell are you talking about?"

Despite the nature of the situation that had called them both out of a warm bed, Santini seemed very amused as he regarded his partner. "I assume it's the cameo lady." Then, before James could make the proper indignant noises or tell him to go to hell, Santini delivered the defining blow. "I can still smell her perfume on you."

James set his jaw hard. The more he protested, the more entertained Santini would be. So he ignored the grin, the words and the assumption. "Give me the details," he growled, nodding at the restaurant.

Santini became all business. "The details are our thieves got a taste of blood last time and decided that they liked it. Or that at least they're not afraid of it and won't let the thought of killing someone else get in the way of their making money the easy way." He nodded at the body bag on the ground. "This is Alice Keller-man, the owner's wife. One bullet to the head," he described grimly. "I guess they decided that it's less complicated robbing the restaurant after closing hours instead of studying the comings and goings of each new place before going in for the kill."

The old M.O. had called for only a week between hits. This one had occurred a couple of days after the last robbery/homicide. Things were stepping up.

James took a minute to look around the vast kitchen where the murder had obviously taken place. The robbers most likely had broken in, surprising the woman and taking her hostage. Maybe they'd needed her to open the safe and then had disposed of her once her usefulness was over.

They were dealing with at least one cold-blooded bastard if not more.

As James crossed to look at the late Mrs. Kellerman, he noticed the dark red smear right where the body had been before the M.E. had finished with it. James squatted down to examine the stain. The bottom of a shoe had made wavy lines right through the middle of the dark pool. One of the robbers had obviously slipped on the victim's blood. Trying to approximate what he took to have happened, James figured the robber had grabbed something to steady himself. Or braced himself against something.

The stainless-steel refrigerator door fit the bill.

He looked at Santini. "I want CSI to dust the refrigerator for prints."

Santini frowned. "We're going to get a hell of a lot of partials off that. The crime lab's not going to be happy, Munro. Everyone in the place and their cousin had to have access to it."

Concentrating, James visualized what must have happened. The robber slipped and his hand automatically went flying out to grab something. That meant he had to have used the refrigerator to brace himself.

"Here," he said, drawing a circle in the air just around the area of interest. "I want them to dust right around here and see what they find. He might have been wearing gloves, but if he wasn't, maybe we finally got lucky."

"In your case, that would make two for tonight, right?" Santini asked innocently as he beckoned over one of the crime-scene investigators.

James glared at him, at a loss how to make the man shut up short of stuffing a sock into his mouth. "You talk too much," he retorted over his shoulder as he went to investigate the small office.

"That's 'cause you don't talk at all," Santini called after him.

They got lucky.

Thorough, the robber had wiped down the refrigerator, but in his hurry, he'd missed a spot. Enough was left behind to provide them with a partial print. Now all that was left was to find another print in the system with sufficient matching points. Their computer people went to work.

With only a few hours left before he was officially on Monday morning duty, James went back to his apartment to grab a quick shower and get a change of clothes. And to hopefully get the scent of Constance off his body. He knew Santini would continue making sly remarks until he did.

That was the easy part. Getting her off his body. Getting her off his mind was going to be the really tricky part and so far, he wasn't succeeding. Even in the midst of the investigation, as he'd paused to look down at the face of the dead woman, he could only thing of Constance. Of the way she'd felt against him, the way her body had urged him on. The way he'd wanted to make love to her all night.

Part of him had really hoped that once he'd made love to her, the novelty, the allure would be over. But he hadn't made love to her, he'd made love *with* her and that made all the difference in the world. The allure, the *need* to make love with her again only intensified. And that only frustrated the hell out of him.

He wanted her now more than ever.

He hated dependency of any kind. He'd never taken up smoking for that very reason and although he did enjoy alcohol, he could walk away from a drink any time. Walking away from her would take concentrated effort. And he wasn't all that sure he could pull it off.

"What are you looking at?" he asked as he placed a bowl of fresh water before Stanley. As if to answer him, the German shepherd made a whining noise, leaving it up to him to interpret. "Sorry, I don't speak dog, although she might," he bit off, thoroughly disgruntled.

Ignoring the water and the food dish, Stanley went over to the sofa and began to sniff around the area. The mournful whining increased.

"Don't you start, too." It was bad enough that James missed her, that he was unsuccessfully wrestling with feelings about her, he didn't need the dog underscoring the fact. "She's not going to come back," he told his pet. "Last night was just a one-time thing."

Stanley cocked his head and eyed him as if he didn't believe what he was saying.

That made two of them, James thought and he was far from happy about it.

The case heated up. After much searching, the database had spit up a match. A small-time hood who'd already been sent away twice for B and E. That would explain his desperation not to be identified. One more conviction and the key would be thrown away.

They had a suspect. And James had an excuse not to pick up the phone and call Constance. He was busy, very busy. He allowed the details of the case to consume his waking moments. If Constance made more than a few appearances in his mind during the course of the investigation, well, nobody needed to know that but him. He certainly wasn't about to say anything to Santini, no matter how much the other man insisted on bombarding him with questions.

The suspect wasn't at his last known address. They

put out an APB on him and combed through all his known haunts. Without any luck.

Each day that passed without any contact with Constance, James counted as a success. But even so, in the back of his mind, he was rather surprised that she hadn't called him.

Maybe she wasn't as pushy as he'd thought.

Or maybe she wasn't as interested as he'd thought.

Or maybe...

Maybe he'd better just enjoy the fact that he was free of her and stop driving himself crazy.

It wasn't possible.

He broke down.

Picking up the phone, James called her apartment the way he had five times before and got her answering machine. Again. And like the five other times, he listened to the soft voice tell him that she couldn't come to the phone right now and for him to leave a message. His body tightened just at the sound of her voice. He felt himself responding in ways that disconcerted him.

James all but threw the receiver back in the cradle before the beep and swore.

That made six times he'd broken down. Six times he'd called in the last couple of days. And six times she hadn't been there to answer the phone.

So where the hell was she? he wondered angrily.

As if in response to his silent question, he heard the sound of small, raised voices in the distance. Children's voices. Coming closer.

All right, he thought, it was official. He'd lost his mind. And then he saw them. And her. They were all being led into the squad room by one of the uniformed officers from downstairs.

What the hell were they doing here?

And didn't she own any loose-fitting clothing? he wondered, staring at the strawberry-colored dress she had on. Why did everything she wear look as if it were making love to her body?

"And this is where the detectives are," Officer Harrelson was saying as the last of Constance's class crossed the threshold.

Heads began to peer over the cubicle walls like jack-in-the-boxes set in slow motion.

"Don't look now, but we're being invaded," Harry Kyle, the oldest member of the squad, announced. Harry had five kids and twelve grandchildren. Pint-sized invasions were nothing new to him. But the incoming class had their sights set on another target.

"Hey, there's Detective Munro," one of the children cried, pointing in James's direction.

The next moment, as if they were one being with thirty-five sets of legs, Constance's fourth graders suddenly converged around his cubicle. The ones who were in the very front managed to pour into the space around his desk while the others lined up behind them, blocking any possible route of escape that might have existed.

"Class, he has work to do," Constance reminded them softly as she worked her way to the front of the group, weaving in and out between the students. Once she made it to the front, she turned and started to move the three invaders back. "What did I say about being quiet and keeping out of everyone's way?"

"That we should do it," Evangeline Hernandez answered importantly.

"Right." Constance swept an expectant look over each and every one of them.

The patrolman assigned to giving her class the tour looked at her with gratitude. It was obvious that Officer Harrelson knew his way around the office better than he did around children.

James thought the man's smile was a shade too friendly and experienced a sharp prick of annoyance. He'd given up assigning different names to the feeling. He felt jealousy and he was just going to deal with it.

As he rose to his feet, he saw Santini approaching. Behind him were several of the other detectives. Suddenly, James's cubicle had become the focal point of the room.

*Great, just what I need,* he thought in mute disgust.

Santini dug out his Italian charm. "Nice to see you again." He took Constance's hand, holding it rather than actually shaking it. "Nick Santini, Munro's partner," he added in case she didn't remember him from her last visit here.

"Yes, I know who you are, Detective," she assured him, her voice wrapping itself around every word like warm hot chocolate on a cold morning. "I'm very good with faces."

"She looks like she'd be very good with everything else, too," James heard one of the detectives behind him murmur under his breath. He turned his head, scanning the space for the guilty party, but he couldn't zero in on anyone in particular. Not that he was short of suspects. To a man, the hard-nosed detectives all looked pretty taken with Constance.

"All these yours?" Santini asked her, indicating the class.

She smiled and nodded. "Every one of them. Finest fourth graders in the city."

There was a fond look in her all-inclusive glance. James could see pride blossoming on each and every one of the small, upturned faces. He would bet each one of them would have gone to hell and back for her.

How did she do it? It was hard enough to keep order in a class this size, much less gain their respect and admiration. She really was a miracle worker in every sense of the word.

Hadn't she worked a miracle on him? Made him remember he had a soul?

The other detectives looked as if they were going to start fawning on her. James took the lead before that happened. "What are you doing here?"

The expression on her face was genial and polite. The same look she'd given Santini. The same one the patrolman had received. Except that Santini and the patrolman hadn't slept with her less than a week ago. He had. Didn't that entitle him to something a little different? To something a little more?

What the hell was wrong with him? He'd purposely stayed away to avoid this very thing. And now he felt slighted because he hadn't received it? He really *was* losing his mind.

Damn it, she made him feel so restless inside, he didn't know if he was coming or going.

"Uncle Bob arranged a field trip for my class," she told him.

"Uncle Bob?" Santini echoed incredulously. "That would be Bob Walker?"

"One and the same," she answered cheerfully. Her warm smile washed over the men one by one, coming to settle on James.

Her smile was enigmatic. He had no idea what she was thinking, what to make of it. Other than acknowledging that she drove him crazy.

"Let's go, class, follow Officer Harrelson," she told them. "There's still a lot to see."

"Can Detective Munro come with us?" one of the girls pleaded.

"Maybe some other time," Constance replied before he could come up with an excuse himself. "Police work takes up a lot of his time."

That stung, he thought, then tried to figure out if she'd meant it to hurt him. Nothing in her manner gave him the slightest clue.

"Where are the bad guys?" one of the students at the front of the line asked as they were being herded away from the detectives.

"In the holding cell," Officer Harrelson told him. "That's downstairs."

Some of the boys turned toward Constance eagerly. "Can we go see that next?"

"Maybe a little later," Constance promised, shepherding the last of them out of the room.

James curbed the desire to follow them. To follow her. To take her aside and ask her where she'd been the last few times he'd called. But that would crack the facade he was trying so hard to maintain.

Still standing by his desk, Santini sighed audibly as the other detectives disbanded and returned to their cubicles.

"That, my friend, is one very fine-looking woman. I swear she gets easier on the eyes every time I see her."

James shot him a warning glance. "You're drooling on my desk."

"Can you blame me?" Santini sighed. "If I wasn't married—"

"She still wouldn't be seen with you," James assured him darkly.

"Why?" There was just a shade of indignation in his voice. "You don't seem to be taking advantage of any opportunities."

Something protective stirred in his chest. "She's not an opportunity."

Santini's expression was nothing if not wistful. "She is from where I'm standing. A golden opportunity to get into heaven."

Sighing, Santini shook his head and went back to his

own cubicle. Leaving James alone with his thoughts. Exactly where he didn't want to be.

When he got off duty, James told himself he was going home. And staying there. He did go home, just long enough to walk Stanley. Then he got back into his car and headed uptown.

He had to hold himself in check to keep from pounding on her door. "What the hell was that about?" he demanded when she finally came to open it.

She stepped back to allow him in. She'd been expecting him ever since this afternoon. "You're going to have to be a little more specific than that, James."

He struggled for a shred of patience. It eluded him. There were things going on inside of him that he couldn't even begin to explain or examine. "What were you doing at the precinct today?"

"I already explained that at the precinct," she reminded him. "I was taking the class on a field trip."

"Why not to the zoo?" he asked. "Or the Museum of Natural History? Or the Museum of Modern Art?" There were so many other places besides the precinct. So many places where he wouldn't be reminded of just how much he missed her.

"Because the students have already been there." She noticed he looked harried. Tired. She wanted to run her fingers along his face to comfort him. She wasn't sure how long she could restrain the impulse. "And, more importantly, because so many of them have members of their families in gangs, I wanted them to see what the inside of a police station looked like without first having to go through a booking. I was hoping to impress them with the strength and intelligence of the people they'd be going up against if they considered slipping into a life of crime." She found it strange to be talking about ten-year-olds this way, but criminal intent took hold early on the mean streets and she intended to out-maneuver it any way she could.

James realized this afternoon hadn't been about him; it had been about them, about her students. The lady was one of a kind.

And all he could think about was how much he'd missed her these last few days. How very much he wanted to be with her.

How much he wanted her.

It got the better of him.

Too weak to resist the flood of feelings that were all but drowning him, James caught her up in his arms and kissed her. Kissed her as if his very soul would expire in the next ten seconds if he didn't.

Because part of him believed that this was true.

## Chapter Fourteen

Even as James swept Constance into his arms, even as the kiss took hold and his head began to spin, he was angry. Angry because he had no say in what was happening to him.

All control had been summarily yanked from him and he was just a puppet, a conduit through which these sensations, these tormenting feelings, traveled. He wanted to be able to walk away at any time, not be held hostage, not feel this gut-wrenching, overwhelming need to make love with this woman fate had put in his path.

Nothing was simple anymore, nothing straightforward. Before Constance, he'd functioned. He did his job, went home, took care of his dog, went to bed. End of story. That had been all he'd required.

Now, now there was this insatiable appetite, these desires, these dreams that gave him no peace, that seemed to complicate every waking and sleeping moment of his life.

Why couldn't he just call an end to it?

He would, he decided. He would. Soon. For his own survival.

But not right now.

Because now was meant for her.

The gentle tempo they'd established by the end of the last time they'd made love had vanished like so many beads of moisture in the August sun. In its place was an urgency even more intense than the very first time they'd made love. It was there, gnawing away at his sensibilities, his restraint, because he knew what was waiting for him, knew the extreme euphoria coming together with her generated in his blood. He was beyond eager to lose himself within its confines.

Within her.

Swiftly, her tank top and shorts found their way to the floor. James stripped off his own shirt and began to shuck his jeans down along his hips when he felt her mouth curving against his.

Was she smiling?

Laughing?

Nerves and insecurity bonded together. Pulling his head back, he eyed Constance quizzically. She *was* smiling.

She framed his face with her hands, loving him so much it physically hurt her heart. The cameo still worked. She had begun to lose faith. "And here I thought you didn't like me anymore."

This was a time for disclaimers, for bailing out. She'd given him a golden opportunity, but he couldn't make himself take it. Not when every fiber of his being was so centered on her.

"Like you?" he rasped, his voice barely squeezing itself out past his emotions. "Lady, I can't get enough of you."

She wrapped her arms, her body, around his, sealing herself to him. Heat flared at all the points that came together, exciting her. The room swam. Her eyes were only on his.

"That's good, because the feeling's very mutual."

Not standing on protocol, she brought her mouth up to his and anything else that might have been said died unspoken.

They let their actions do the talking for them.

He caressed her over and over again, stroking her silken skin, memorizing the soft curves and gentle dips her body took. Familiarizing himself with every inch of her. Because he knew in his heart that this was going to have to last him a very long time.

As she began to reciprocate, he thought he was going to lose what little grip he still had over himself. A moment later, when her fingers took possession of him, desire slammed against him so hard it all but jarred his teeth loose. Digging deep within himself, he somehow found the strength to hold back a little while longer. Even when she began to slide her fingertips down the length of him, he managed.

Just.

But he was only human and there were limits. James caught hold of her wrist, stilling her fingers, his eyes warning her to stop. When she looked at him, dazed, he took the opportunity to reverse their positions, pushing her down flat on her back. She wiggled beneath him in tantalizing anticipation.

Wanting her to remember this as the best time, he showed her just how many ways a woman could be driven to the brink and over, only to be brought back and taken there again.

She understood now the definition of sweet agony. She lost count of how many times she'd felt the explosions. Her body was quivering beneath his. Slick, exhausted. And somehow, miraculously, still wanting. But that was his doing because she wanted to become one with him again.

She hardly had the strength to slip her arms around his neck as he moved back up to face her.

"If…your…goal's…death…by…passion…you've… almost…succeeded." Constance managed to get the statement out in single-word increments.

He raised himself over her, the heat from his body searing into hers. Nearly singeing them both. She felt like home to him. A very dangerous feeling, he warned himself, because that meant he was putting his fate in someone else's hands. As a detective, as a man, he'd learned he could only be burned that way.

"No goals."

It was a promise. He couldn't let himself have goals, not when it came to a woman. That was beyond his realm. Beyond his sphere of trust. Eli might have had something special with his wife of forty-three years, but that was just it. Special. Rare.

James didn't see himself as the kind of man who believed he was entitled to something special. And nothing short of that would work. Besides, he knew he wasn't the easiest man to get along with. Someone really special would have to put up with him and not run exasperated and screaming from the room.

None of that mattered right now.

Because the next moment, he was sliding into her, letting the last of his thoughts go to wherever it was that they went when people unwound.

His hands threaded through hers and he raised them over her head. Meeting her eyes, he never looked away as he started to move within her.

He heard her sharp intake of breath as she wrapped her legs around him, felt the urgency of her movement as it became one with his.

They raced together, driving up the tempo until it engulfed them.

Until it brought them what they wanted.

Because he knew that he couldn't allow himself to see her again after tonight, he let the euphoria overtake him, blotting out his mind. It took him a while before he could regulate his breathing. He was acutely aware that her breasts were moving up and down at an accelerated pace.

She was having her own trouble with her breathing. Combing back her hair with his hand, taking away anything that might begin to obstruct his view of her, he asked, "Did I remember to say hi?"

Her eyes crinkled. She moved just a touch to watch his reaction to her. "No, I don't believe you did."

"Hi."

He watched as a smile began in her eyes and filtered down to her mouth, encompassing all of her. Encompassing him.

"Hi," she responded.

He knew he should be getting up, making some excuse in order to leave. But all he could do was put his arm around her and pull her closer to him on the rug.

Over in the corner, Felicia mercifully continued sleeping, unmindful of the passion she'd just missed.

Constance's breathing grew steadier. She loved the feeling of being tucked against him. Loved feeling his warmth just beneath her cheek.

Raising her head, she placed her hand on his chest and looked at him. Mischief highlighted her mouth. "So, how about those Mets?"

He laughed shortly. "You want to talk stats?"

Lacing her fingers together on his chest, she rested her chin on them, her eyes intent on his. "I want to talk about anything you want to talk about. I just want to hear the sound of your voice."

He combed his fingers through her hair. Even that sent a shaft of desire through him. There was no end to this feeling, was there? "You make it hard for a man to walk away."

Something tightened inside of her, bracing. She'd been abandoned before. By people who had no choice in the matter. Neither one of her parents had wanted to die and leave her. And there had been nothing she could do to change the situation, to prevent it.

But she could here.

Somehow, she had to find the way to make him want to stay. The way she needed him to.

"Then don't." She saw the wary look that entered his eyes and thought she understood what was behind it. "No strings, James. I'm not asking for a commitment. I'm just asking you to stay. And be my friend."

He laughed then, hooking his arm around her waist. "You treat all your friends this way?"

She tried to keep a straight face. "Just the very, very special ones."

"And just how big is this 'special' club?" Even as he asked, he felt a silver of jealousy piercing his skin. It was irrational, but he didn't want there to be others. He wanted her all for himself. And yet, he was trying to walk away.

This was confusing the hell out of him.

"Just one member." She shifted, her hair brushing along his chest. "You." Her lips lightly grazed his, then pulled back. Her voice grew lower. Seductive. "Are you planning on talking all night?"

No, what he wanted to do all night, all eternity, was make love with her.

It convinced him, once and for all, that she truly was a witch.

"You were the one who said she wanted to hear the sound of my voice," he reminded her.

"True," she acknowledged. "But everything in its place."

Then, before he could answer, Constance brought her mouth within an inch of his again. Tempting him. It seemed incredible, given that they had just made love, but there he had it. She was tempting him.

And he was unable to resist.

Pulling her to him, he kissed her long and hard, with all the passions that she had unearthed within him.

And the dance began again.

James sat up, his long legs swinging over the right side of the four-poster bed, the sheet just barely pooling at his waist. Echoes of midnight filled the corners of the sumptuous bedroom where Constance lay asleep beside him.

He was getting further and further entrenched.

The thought throbbed within his brain.

Instead of ending it the night after she and her class had invaded his precinct, he'd somehow found himself coming back again and again, under one pretext or another. Always for one more time before the end.

And the end kept slipping another notch away.

He dragged his hand through his hair, trying to anchor himself. Trying to find strength. He couldn't allow this to go on. He knew the consequences. Knew that he and Constance would wind up walking the path he and Janice had. The same path his parents had. At some point in time, probably soon, they would be standing in the middle of a battle zone, taking aim at one another, wondering where all the good feelings had gone.

He needed to go before that happened.

It was the only way he could preserve the memory of what they'd shared. He needed to go now before her eyes made him stay. He had to fade away from her like smoke rings in the dark.

She never fully slept when he was next to her. On some level, she was always aware of his body beside hers. Aware when he shifted away. Sleep receded entirely as she felt the bed moving, felt the slight tug on her sheet as he began to rise.

Something inside of her knew he wasn't just getting up to visit to the bathroom. He was leaving. A genteel lady of Southern breeding would have let him.

But she wasn't a lady. She was a woman in love. Hopelessly in love with a man who lit up everything around her like the Fourth of July. Slowly turning, she saw him begin to gather his clothes. Last night they'd made love as if they belonged together. Deliberately, unhurried and with familiarity. They made love as if this was going to continue.

Even as the thought echoed in her brain, she'd warned herself not to grow too complacent. There was a danger in that.

And she'd been right.

She fingered the cameo, drawing on the strength of its original owner. A woman who had never given up believing her love would return to her, even in the face of total and utter hopelessness.

"Don't leave," she whispered.

His back to her, James stopped. She'd spoken so softly, for a second he'd thought it was just his imagination tormenting him. But when he turned around, he saw that she was awake. And looking at him.

Guilt pressed down on his chest like a huge boulder. "Constance, I've got to—"

She refused to listen, refused to let him tell her that he had to leave. The phone hadn't summoned him back to work. And there was no other excuse she'd willingly accept. He was afraid of what was growing between them. So was she. But not so afraid that she would back away from it.

"Come back to bed," she coaxed, throwing back the sheet from his side.

Her nude body pressed against the mattress, issuing a silent invitation to him.

Unable to refuse her, James let his clothes drop to the floor again. Without a word, he slid back into bed beside her. To make love with her again.

Morning arrived to mock him, pushing the light of day into all the secret corners of his soul.

He knew what he had to do.

They were in the kitchen and she wore a long silk

robe that insisted on opening up at all the wrong moments, tantalizing him. Making him acutely aware that she had on nothing beneath. And that he wanted that body with the same insatiable desire he'd had the night before.

But something about the morning fortified him. Kept him strong and on the path he knew he had to take.

"I'm no good for you, Constance."

Standing with her back to him at the counter, she tried not to stiffen.

*Here it comes.*

Turning, she filled his coffee cup and then set the coffee pot back on the burner.

She kept her smile in place even though nerves scrambled madly inside of her. "Why don't you let me be the judge of what's good for me? I've been doing it longer than you have."

He wasn't going to let her reason him out of what he knew was right. Because if he did, someday in the not-too-distant future, she would begin to hate him, see his flaws until there was nothing else. And nights like last night would be nothing more than a memory.

He wrapped his hands around the coffee cup, but didn't drink. "I don't have a clue how to make a relationship work."

There was a hollow feeling in the middle of her chest, as if a cannonball had just gone through. "I thought we were doing rather well. Relationships don't come with blueprints, James. They're like snowflakes. Each one's different."

He thought of the first complaint that Janice had hurled at him. It was something he couldn't help. "I'm a private person. I don't open up."

"I don't plan on vivisecting you, I plan on listening if you want to talk."

"It's not going to work," he insisted. He had to leave now, before he couldn't. Before he watched himself destroy what they had, the way his parents had destroyed what they'd had.

Constance caught her bottom lip between her teeth. A sob bubbled up in her throat and she struggled to keep it at bay. She wasn't going to use tears to keep him, that wouldn't be fair.

She already knew that she loved this scarred man who had so much good in him. But she couldn't make him love her, couldn't make him stay. That was his decision. Anything less wouldn't count.

Just this once she wished she could fight dirty.

Feeling utterly numb, as if her body suddenly didn't belong to her, she nodded slowly. "If that's the way you feel."

"That's the way I feel."

That was the way he *had* to feel, he told himself as he walked out the door. For his own good. And most importantly, for hers.

Life before Constance had been trying at times. Life after he left her became a living hell. Both for him and, he suspected, for the people around him.

A dark mood came over him the likes of which he

was unacquainted with. It spread around him like an inky cloak, its edges touching everyone who came in contact with him. He snapped off heads wherever he went.

As his partner, Santini tried hard to kid him out of his state, then tried to lecture and nag him out of it. Nothing worked. Nothing penetrated the barrier James had installed around himself. In self-defense, Santini backed off. People in the precinct kept out of his way, waiting to ride out the storm.

The storm only intensified and gave no signs of coming to an end.

Its drastic consequences and possible immortality became evident the morning he and Santini finally caught up with the suspect in the restaurant robberies. Brought to a run-down motel in an equally run-down part of the city by a tip from an informant, James and Santini brought several uniformed police officers with them.

After hurrying up three flights, they rushed the room, guns drawn and ready. The suspect's attempt to flee via the fire escape was quickly foiled. He was taken down. Desperate, he attempted to bargain his way down to a lesser offense than murder by offering up the name of his accomplices. A statement, sanctioned by the assistant district attorney, was taken. The string of restaurant robberies known as R Squared came to an end. As far as James, Santini and the rest of the squad were concerned, the case was closed.

Every time a case was over, he'd feel some measure

of triumph over a job well done. He didn't need the chief's verbal reinforcement, he just felt it.

That feeling of accomplishment was missing this time. There was no sense of accomplishment, no sense of pride. Nothing. Only that same twisted feeling in his gut he had been living with for over a week. The same kind of feeling he'd experienced when he'd found his brother lying lifeless on the bathroom floor.

At the end of the day, he turned down Santini's invitation to celebrate at the local saloon where all the police officers converged to wind down before going home to their families. The sound of their voices would only irritate him.

Everything irritated him.

He couldn't find a place for himself and seriously began to doubt that he ever would. Began to doubt that there even *was* a place for him in the world. Ever since he could remember, he'd been essentially an emotional nomad. The only haven he'd ever found...

No, he wasn't going there, he upbraided himself. Not even mentally. He'd put that behind himself and it was going to stay there. Not wanting to go home to his apartment, but unwilling to join Santini and the others, he went to the only place he could.

Eli's.

The ancient bell heralded his entrance.

Behind the counter, Eli was trying to read a label on a can, holding it out at various lengths, searching for an elusive focal point. The sound of the bell made him look up.

The day-old whiskers on his thin cheeks spread out in a smile.

"Finally, he comes." He put the can down. His eyebrows narrowed into a fuzzy line above his nose. "And he didn't bring her with him."

James went over to the first aisle and took down two boxes of spaghetti. Nothing ever changed, he thought. Eli had been putting the same things in the same places ever since he could remember. There was a comfort in that. "People are going to put you away, old man, if you keep talking to yourself."

"I wasn't talking to myself." Eli leaned over the counter so that his voice would carry as James went down another aisle. "I was talking to you. Poetic license," he explained. He shook his head as James approached him. "Still thin." And then he asked almost eagerly, "How did your lady like Felicia?"

"She's not my lady and Felicia has a good home."

Eli snorted as James deposited the jar of sauce and two boxes on the counter. "Too bad you don't. You look like hell."

James moved his shoulders in a careless shrug. "It's the job."

Eli seemed unconvinced. "It's something else. You and she have a fight?"

"There is no me and her."

The warning look in James's eyes had no effect on Eli. "What happened?"

"I broke it off."

A knowing expression came over Eli's face. He nodded his head. "Before she walked out on you." James shot him a dark look. "Don't give me that look, you stand behind this counter for forty-six years, you learn a few things. Like people will do anything to avoid pain. Even cause it themselves because they think it'll hurt less. It doesn't," he said with conviction. "It hurts just the same. More." Without ringing the items up, he deposited them into a bag and threw in a box of chocolate-chip cookies that were on the counter. "Now stop being such a jackass and ask her to forgive you before she comes to her senses."

Eli pushed the bag toward him, then came around the counter, concern etched on his thin face despite his flippant tone. "Contrary to popular opinion, love doesn't happen to everyone, Jimmy."

James balked. He should have known better than to come here. Eli was worse than Santini. "Who said anything about love?"

"You did," Eli insisted, refusing to back down despite the darkening expression on James's face. "Everything about you shouts that you're heartsick. You don't get that way unless you're in love."

Annoyed, at the end of his rope as well as his patience, James dismissed the man's words. "That's beside the point."

"Beside the point?" Eli cried incredulously. "Beside the point? Jimmy, that *is* the point. Of everything. Nothing else is worthwhile without that." He pushed him toward the door. "Now go, get her back."

James looked back at the counter. "My groceries—"

"You can come back for them later. With her." Having delivered his final word on the subject, Eli pushed James out the door.

## Chapter Fifteen

Constance blew out a long breath and then took an equally long sip of diet soda. The sides of the can had gone from chilled to warm and the bubbles inside had long since departed. She hardly noticed.

She couldn't keep her mind on her work.

It certainly wasn't because the work was taxing. But she'd reread the same seven-word sentence half a dozen times now and it just wasn't sinking in.

Nothing was sinking in.

That was because it couldn't. Disappointment had filled up every available space inside of her while making it feel as if everything was collapsing. She'd been so sure, so very sure that there was a connection between James and her. So sure that despite his demeanor and his obvious desire to retain his brooding persona, he was her soul mate.

Soul mates didn't have to be identical copies of one another, they had to supply what the other person lacked. Had to make the other person feel complete just by their very existence. And he had. James had made her feel complete.

Somehow, he had been what was missing in her life. She'd felt whole with him. Safe. And so incredibly sexy, as if sensuality shot out every pore whenever she was with him. No one had ever made her feel like that before.

And no one was ever going to make her feel like that again. Because she just wasn't going to go through this a second time. The grieving, the emptiness, the pain just wasn't worth it. Better not know any of it than to stand around, torn and bleeding, waiting for the inevitable to happen. Because it always did.

The cameo was a fraud. There was no happily-ever-after, no reward for believing. She wished she'd never believed in it.

Restless, unable to fit inside her own skin, she sighed. She'd felt upset and used when she'd broken it off with Josh, but the loss, well, the loss hadn't really touched her. What she'd mourned more than anything was the idea of losing love rather than actually losing Josh. If she were being honest, he had never set her soul on fire. Not once.

But James had. Every time.

There was no other way to describe what had gone down between James and her except to say that the forces of nature were involved. This had been a whirlwind thing, taking away her breath, accelerating her heart rate. She felt the way she'd always dreamed about feeling. In love. Wildly, hopelessly in love.

And now those same adjectives could be used to describe the despair that was closing in around her. She was vainly trying to hold it at bay.

Constance knew without being told that she was facing a losing battle.

She *had* to snap out of it.

She had to stop feeling sorry for herself and get back out among the living. He wasn't going to appear magically on her doorstep to make things right. Even she wasn't naive enough to believe that.

"I suppose I'm just going to have to get on with it, go through the five stages of grief, or however many there are, right Felicia?"

The dog, curled up at her feet like a small hairy comforter, barely raised her head in acknowledgment of the words. Even the dog wasn't listening, she thought in annoyance.

"Wait, just wait until it happens to you. Wait until you meet that drop-dead German shepherd hunk who'll start you dreaming big dreams and then just when he has you in the palm of his paw, he'll walk away. Not a pretty picture, I guarantee it."

She bent over and scratched the animal behind her ear. The simple action helped to soothe her. As for the animal, if Felicia were any more relaxed, Constance was certain she'd have to place the dog in a bowl to keep her from floating away.

Constance frowned at the lack of support from the puppy. "I promise to be more sympathetic to you than you are to me right now."

Felicia barely made a sound as she lowered her head back down on her paws, her body still covering her mistress's feet.

Constance did her best to rally. The evening was still young, even if she felt a million years old. "C'mon, Constance," she said sternly. "Snap out of it. You've got book reports to read."

The next moment, Felicia came alive as if someone had suddenly stepped on her tail. But instead of barking, Felicia made a mad dash for the front door. Her tail was wagging so wildly, it looked as if it were in danger of screwing right off.

Constance put down her pen and gave up all pretense of working. Maybe later she could get her head together, but right now, her brain cells were scattered in a hundred different directions. And somehow, they all led back to him.

Felicia was still at the front door. "What is it, Lassie? Did Timmie fall down into the well again?" The puppy began to scratch at the bottom of the door. Nobody had rung the bell. "Someone there, girl?" Constance sighed, getting up. "Okay, be that way." Unable to concentrate anyway, she crossed to the front door to check out what had Felicia so excited.

* * *

He'd been standing at her door for five minutes now, mentally arguing with himself.

It wasn't going well.

Even after Eli had literally pushed him out of the store, James had had no intention of coming here. He'd meant to stick to his decision to push on with his life and try somehow to lock away all these unsettling feelings that Constance had unearthed within him.

To do that, he needed to get over Constance.

But then it struck him as he was driving away from Eli's store that if he had to spend this much energy trying to get over her, he'd already failed in his initial resolve not to fall for her in the first place. In leaving her, he wasn't protecting himself from possible future heartache, he was ushering it in early. Of his own volition.

Just as Eli had pointed out.

It made no sense.

Neither did being without her when she hadn't pushed him away. So he'd turned the car around and instead of going home, he'd headed uptown.

The full head of steam he'd gathered had remained with him until just a few minutes ago, when he'd found himself standing before her door. And his future.

What if she didn't want to see him anymore? What if he'd alienated her so badly that she'd gone on to see someone else, someone from that vast crowd of people she knew?

What if…?

His mind ceased raising questions whose sole purpose was to torment him the second the door opened and he saw Constance standing in the doorway. She was dressed in another pair of impossibly short white shorts and a nonexistent sky-blue halter top that showed off all her best features.

No, that wasn't right, he mentally corrected himself. Constance's very best feature was her heart.

Everything else ran a close second and it was all there, hiding beneath thin cotton material, daring him to touch. To take.

Constance's impossible blue eyes widened with surprise as she looked at him, trapping his soul. He wanted her so much, it hurt to breathe. Scared him. Big time.

With effort, he scrambled to cover up what he was positive had to be evident in his eyes and on his face. So he scowled at her. "You didn't even ask who was there. Do you realize I could have pushed my way into your apartment and attacked you right there, inches past your threshold?"

She could have said a lot of things in response to his verbal assault. She could have pretended to be flippant or indifferent. Or she could have shouted at him that he had no right to come in here and throw his weight around. She was entitled to all of that.

But all she could think of was how happy she was to see him. And that maybe, just maybe, her mother hadn't been wrong about the cameo after all.

"Sounds good to me," she told him.

She was taking the wind out of his sails. "Seriously,"

he fumed even as he felt every inch of his body responding to her. Felt his very mind responding to her.

"Seriously," she whispered. "And in the event that it wasn't you at the door, this nice police detective gave me this really fierce attack dog." She looked down at Felicia, who was busy licking his shoes, her tail still going a hundred miles a minute, thumping against the floor like a drum soloist in the spotlight.

Because he wanted to fill his arms with her, James stooped down and picked up the dog instead. Felicia began licking his face. "What's she going to do, knock me over with the breeze created by her tail?"

"The robber would have never expected that."

Rescuing him from Felicia and her pink tongue, which was furiously separating him from the skin on his face, Constance took the dog and pushed her door open all the way with her back.

Once he was inside, Constance put Felicia down on the floor and gently swatted the dog's behind. Trained, though reluctant, Felicia returned to the giant throw pillow in the middle of the room and lay down.

Constance struggled to contain the joy that was trying desperately to break out and take over. Knowing James, there could very well have been some miserably logical reason why he was here and it wasn't because he'd missed her one tenth as much as she had him.

She braced herself for disappointment. "So, what are you doing here?"

He'd asked himself the same question, over and over again, as he'd stared at her door. And had finally come up with an answer just as she'd opened it. "Trying to go home."

"And what, you lost your way?" Constance pushed her hands into her back pockets to keep from throwing them around his neck and dragging him down to her level so she could kiss him until they were both numb. "You live on the other side of town, remember?"

"No, that's where I put away the occasional groceries I buy, where I feed my dog and keep my clothes," he told her quietly. "But that's not home. I haven't had a home. Not really." He was saying things to her he'd never said to anyone else. And realized that he wanted her to know the truth. "Not ever." He thought of his marriage and how he'd felt at first. "I thought I did for a while, but even then, there was this feeling that it wasn't permanent, that things would change." He looked off into space. "And they did."

The temptation to stop, to leave, loomed again before him.

No, he wasn't going to turn tail and run. He'd never been a coward. Never let himself be a coward, but now he knew that he had been just that with her. Because he wouldn't allow himself to admit what he'd been feeling. Wouldn't admit it to himself, much less to her.

But that was behind him now.

Constance pressed her lips together, afraid to push forward. Knowing she had to. "And this home you've suddenly found, where is it?"

He looked at her for a long moment. So long, she thought he wasn't going to answer.

And then he did.

"Wherever you are."

The three words stole her breath away. At the very most, she'd expected him to say he regarded her apartment as his home. She'd never remotely expected him to say her. The second the words registered, Constance could feel tears welling up in her eyes. The tears she hadn't let herself shed all this last week as she'd struggled to hang on to the tiny bits and pieces of hope.

She'd even reread the dusty old diary she'd uncovered as a young girl in the attic of the house they used to live in back in Virginia. Amanda's diary. Amanda had hung on to her belief that her lover was returning to her even when everything had pointed against it. When her parents had tried to marry her off to someone else, she'd stubbornly refused to obey, saying she belonged only to Will. She'd hung on to her hope even as the days, then the months after the war had multiplied. She'd never given up.

But Will had told her he loved her. James had never made any such declaration.

Until now.

She could feel the inside of herself filling with sunbeams. They scattered the tears. "And it took you this long to realize it?"

"That," he allowed, then added, "and a kick in the pants." Constance looked at him quizzically. He elaborated just a little. "Everybody at the precinct began to complain."

She laughed and he remembered how much he loved

that sound. "That you weren't your normally, sunny self?"

"That I was even a worse pain in the butt to deal with than usual." They'd used far more descriptive, forceful words than that, but for her sake, he cleaned it up.

She was trying to connect the dots. He'd mentioned a kick in the rear. "So they escorted you here?"

"No, actually they backed off," he admitted. "Tried to avoid me as much as possible. Even Santini gave up and he never gives up."

"Then what gave you that kick in the pants?"

He'd spent most of his life being closemouthed, resenting having to explain himself, even to his parents on those rare occasions when they hadn't been swiping at one another. Yet answering her felt right. As if he needed to share all this with someone, finally. "Two things really. First, we closed the R-Squared cases."

"Congratulations," she told him, interrupting. "You must feel very relieved."

The careless shrug rolled off his shoulders. "That's just it, I didn't. I didn't feel anything." The next took a great deal to admit, because it made him human. And vulnerable. "It was like I was hollow inside."

*Just like me,* she thought.

"And Eli threw me out of his store."

"Eli?" He hadn't mentioned that name to her before. It didn't belong to any of the detectives in his squad. Uncle Bob had gotten her a complete roster.

James nodded. "The old man who's responsible for everything I am. For me taking the course in life that I did."

An uncle? A mentor? Questions popped up in her head like mushrooms on a lawn after a spring rain. But she knew she had to proceed cautiously. She had his trust for the moment and she didn't want to lose it by saying the wrong thing. But she didn't want to stay in the dark about him any longer.

"He gave you advice?"

He grinned. "No, he let me save his life. And for the first time in mine, I felt good. Really good. Like what I had done really mattered."

He supposed his narrative had left some gaping holes. He tried to fill them in quickly. Later he'd give her more details, but for now, he just wanted to get on with his story. And reach his conclusion.

"I'd left home, worked my way cross country and was living in doorways. Eli and his wife owned this little mom-and-pop grocery store on the Lower East Side. I was in it for the first time one night, contemplating robbing him when someone beat me to it. The guy had a gun and he was threatening to shoot Eli's wife. I was around the corner and nobody saw me," he explained. He loved the way she listened, as if every inch of her were intent on finding out what he had to say. "I don't even remember thinking about it, I just jumped the guy. Eli said I'd saved their lives. But he and his wife gave me a place to stay and sent me to school. So I guess they pretty much saved my life." He was convinced of that. "And now you've joined the club."

She blinked. It was some leap from there to here. "I have?"

It was going to be all right, he told himself. Somehow, he was going to make this right if it wasn't at this very moment. He took her into his arms. And realized just how acutely he'd missed the feel of having her against him.

"Yeah, because being with you kept me from just giving way to despair. You added colors into my life, Constance. Blues and reds, yellows and pinks."

Her eyes crinkled. She hooked her arms around him. "You don't strike me as a pink kind of guy."

"Not on its own, but in concert with the other colors…" He realized that she'd taken him off course. Again. She had a way of making him forget everything else except her. "The point is, you make me feel alive. You make me want to stay alive. It didn't much matter before."

She could feel her heart swelling with happiness. But she needed more. She needed to hear every single word he had to spare. "And it does now?"

He inclined his head. "It does as long as I can stay alive around you."

"I highly recommend it," she told him with enthusiasm, then made a face. "Keeping dead people around is kind of creepy."

He laughed and shook his head. Life with her was never going to be dull. But she had to be made aware of something before he went any further. Before he allowed himself to believe it was all going to be good. That was a trap too many people fell into. Not being prepared.

"You know, what I said the other day's still true. I *don't* know how to make a relationship work."

She took his face between her hands and lightly kissed him on the mouth. Sweetness spiraled right through him, boring down to his very core.

"That's because it's not a one-man job. It's like a see-saw," she explained. "One person can't make it work properly. It takes two to make it work right. And I'm more than willing to take my place on the other end of the seesaw."

Humor quirked his mouth. "I thought you said relationships were like snowflakes."

She waved her hand, dismissing what he presented as a discrepancy. "That was before. This is now. Keep up."

"I'll try, Constance, I surely will try." He toyed with her hair, then let the strand drop. The side of her neck, just above the cameo's black velvet ribbon, presented a very tempting target. He could almost taste her skin. "I'd like to think I have forever to do it, though."

"What do you mean?"

She looked startled. Was he wrong after all? Was this just temporary to her? No strings, no rules? "That didn't come out right, did it?"

She knew better than to shoot him down. "That depends on what you're trying to say."

Okay, this one was for all the marbles, he thought. All or nothing. He didn't know how to play any other way. "I'm trying to say I love you and I want you to marry me, Constance."

It took her a moment. She had to drag the air back into her lungs again. "I think you just said it."

He looked at her, waiting. "Aren't you supposed to say something here?"

Her expression was innocent. "You mean like I love you and I want to marry you, too?"

He nodded, trying not to let her see how he was hanging out on a limb until she gave him the answer he needed. "That sounds about right." He paused. She was doing this to him on purpose. "Well, do you?"

Rather than answer, she made an observation. "Always the interrogator."

"Can't help it." If she was going to say no, he decided, she would have done so by now. She was just stretching this out to get even with him. "It's my police training."

"For the record, Detective, I love and want to marry you, too." She threaded her arms around his neck, bringing her body in to his. "We'd better get started on your husband training then." She grinned at him. "Lesson one, always follow up proposals with a kiss."

He pretended to think before answering. "I can do that."

"You'd better," she laughed. "Or I'll have to trade you in."

He ran his finger over the oval at her throat. "Sorry, only one hit from the cameo per customer."

Amusement danced in her eyes. "Since when did you become such an expert on my family heirloom?"

"Not an expert, exactly. I just write some of the rules as I go along."

She raised her eyes to his expectantly. "About lesson one…"

He pulled her to him, feeling very nuance, every curve. And telling himself that from here on in, his life was finally going to take a turn for the better. Because she was going to be in it.

He blessed the day he found that cameo. Or rather, the woman he'd stumbled over who'd found the cameo. "Coming up."

As he began to lower his mouth to hers, an image registered on his brain and he stopped just short of kissing her.

"Change your mind?" she asked.

"Constance, who's that?" He pointed to the portrait of an older woman she had hanging on the far wall. He'd never noticed it before.

Turning, Constance glanced to where James was pointing. "Oh, that's Amanda Deveaux. The original owner of the cameo. It was done a few years before she died." Puzzled, she looked at him curiously. "Why this sudden interest?"

To his trained eye, that the woman in the portrait was a dead ringer for the old woman he'd run into the morning the cameo had come into his life.

But to his logical mind, he knew it was impossible.

As impossible as finding someone to love when he wasn't looking.

He realized this was how a believer was born. But all that was for another time. He had something better to do with his lips right now than tell tales.

"No reason," he told her. "Just getting to know the family."

Before she could ask anything more, he kissed her. And everything else faded away.

## Epilogue

*May 2, 1867*

"Amanda, it's not safe for you here," Savannah O'Brien stated for what seemed like the tenth time. "Come move into town with us. Mother already has. Frasier and I have more than enough room now that he's added on the extra floor." She smiled at her sister, knowing how much Amanda doted on the two-year-old. "You can help me take care of Patrick."

Amanda sensed her safety was not the only reason behind her sister's offer. Belinda Deveaux had become more and more difficult since her husband's death. "And Mother."

Savannah inclined her head, conceding the point. "And Mother." Amanda had always been more clever than her. But that did not change the fact that she was worried about Amanda, living here alone with only the help to turn to.

Amanda rose from her seat, restless. The porch creaked beneath her feet. They'd had these talks before. "Thank you, but no. My place is here."

"Here?" Savannah cried incredulously. "Amanda, the plantation is crumbling. You have no one to work the fields."

She took offense for the loyal souls who stuck by her when they did not have to. "I have Old Jacob, and Simon and Tess and their children."

"Seven people. And they could leave at any time. Or die." Crossing to her, Savannah placed her gloved hands on her sister's thin arms. She wasn't eating enough, Savannah thought. "Amanda, please. I know why you're staying, but he's not coming." Forcing Amanda to look at her, she repeated, "Will's not coming back. The war's been over for almost two years now. If he were alive, he'd already be here." Amanda pulled away from her. "Darling, it breaks my heart to see you like this."

"He promised me, Savannah. Will promised he'd come back."

"I know, and he would have kept his promise if he could, but Amanda, we lost a lot of good men in that awful war. You have to move on. Please."

But Amanda shook her head. "No, little sister, I have

to wait. I gave him my word." She drew herself up within her shabby dress, as regal as a queen. Hooking her arm through Savannah's, she led her sister from the porch to the wagon that stood waiting to bring her back into town. "I thank you for your offer and your concern, but I am fine." She helped Savannah into the wagon, then handed her the reins. "Say hello to Mother for me."

There was nothing left to do but leave. Savannah shook her head and sighed. "You know where to find us if you change your mind."

Yes, Amanda thought as she watched the wagon pull away, she knew where to find her sister. And her nephew and her mother.

But it was Will she wanted to know where to find.

Amanda ran her hands along her arms. The air was getting chilly. Evening was coming.

Heartsick, not knowing what to do with herself, she went down to the road that she watched so anxiously each day.

"Oh, Will," she whispered to the emptiness that surrounded her, "please come home. I am so weary, so very weary of trying to hold on."

She had valiantly held on to her hope even as her mother had tried to browbeat her into marrying Frasier, telling her that he was far more interested in her than he was in her sister. Each day she'd had to endure her mother's recriminations and taunting. It was her love for Will that had sustained her.

But now, she was losing her grasp. Was he never coming home? Was she a fool to hope?

She stood at the fence, the way she did each evening, no matter what the weather, and willed him to appear.

"Please, please, please come back to me."

She stared intently, praying, repeating the words over and over again.

But there was nothing, just the way there had been yesterday, and the day before that and the day before that. The road remained empty.

"Miss Amanda, come back inside, it's starting to rain." She didn't have to turn around to see who it was. Old Jacob had come looking for her. Old Jacob had been her father's body servant. And now he cleaved to her. He was scolding her the way he had when she was very young and willful. "Maybe Mr. Will will be here tomorrow."

She smiled at the old man, grateful for his part in the game she played with herself.

"Maybe," she agreed. And then she saw Old Jacob squinting at something over her shoulder. Her heart scrambled up to her throat. "What is it?"

Old Jacob was far taller than she was. Did he see something that she couldn't?

Someone?

"Oh mah lawd." Shocked, the old man's eyes opened so wide they looked as if they would fall out of his very head.

"What, what do you see?" she cried anxiously. Even

as she asked, she swung around and began running down the empty road. The mists were turning into rain. She didn't care.

"Miss Amanda, no."

There were marauders on the road. Carpetbaggers and drifters who robbed those who had next to nothing to call their own. But she didn't think about that. She only thought about Will. It had to be Will. It *had* to be.

And then she saw him.

A lone, bearded figure half staggering, half walking, coming down the road.

He was barely more than a shadow. A shadow in a tattered Confederate uniform.

Her heart recognized what her mind was still trying to comprehend.

A cry tore loose from her throat. "Will!"

At the sound of his name, the man's head rose. His dazed eyes sharpened. Disbelief slowly took possession of his features, as if he could not believe that he had finally come to journey's end after all these many endless days of walking.

"Oh my God, Will!" Catching her skirt up in her hands, she raced toward him, half-afraid that she was hallucinating.

But Old Jacob had seen him, too, so this could *not* be just a figment of her imagination. Will had to be real. Dear God, he was real.

Reaching him, Amanda threw her arms around Will.

He felt so thin, so weak. Surprise and dismay echoed in her voice as he sagged against her.

"Jacob," she called out to the man in the background, "bring water. I need water. And bread!"

The old man needed no more. He hurried to the house to bring back what she required.

She could feel her heart swelling. From joy. From concern. "You came back to me," she cried.

He needed to touch her, to run his blistered, scarred fingers along her soft skin and assure himself that he wasn't having another one of his dreams.

"They left me for dead, Amanda. At Gettysburg, they left me for dead. But all I could think about was getting back to you. You brought me back from the grave, Amanda. You were all I could think about. I'm sorry it took me so long."

She could hardly see for the tears. They spilled freely down her face. She didn't bother brushing them away. Both her hands were needed to hold him up. "All that matters is that you're here."

He took a deep breath, trying to gather strength from somewhere. Will focused on her neck. "You still have the cameo."

"I never took it off. I was afraid if I did, something would happen to you."

He straightened as best he could and took the woman he loved more than life into his arms. Trying not to sag against her. "You kept me safe, Amanda. Your love kept me safe."

"Love kept us both safe," she whispered. And then she kissed him the way she'd been waiting almost six years to do.

Everything else melted away when she did.

\* \* \* \* \*

*Don't miss Marie Ferrarella's next story,*
*SUNDAYS ARE FOR MURDER, available*
*January 2006 from Signature Spotlight.*

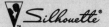

# SPECIAL EDITION™

Divorce was tough enough on
Shawn Fletcher—selling the house and
watching her ex remarry really stung.
So a flirtation with her daughter's math
teacher, Matt McFarland, was a nice
surprise. But how would her daughter—
and the Callie's Corner Café gang—
take the news?

Look for

# A PERFECT LIFE
### by Patricia Kay

available January 2006

**Coming soon from**
**CALLIE'S CORNER CAFÉ**

IT RUNS IN THE FAMILY—February 2006
SHE'S THE ONE—March 2006

*Where love comes alive*™

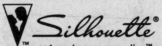

# Silhouette

# SPECIAL EDITION™

### The second story in
### The Moorehouse Legacy!

# HIS COMFORT AND JOY
## by Jessica Bird
### January 2006

Sweet, small-town Joy Moorehouse knew
getting tangled up in fantasies about political
powerhouse Gray Bennett was ridiculous.

Until he noticed her...really noticed her.

### Alex Moorehouse's story will be available April 2006.

4 1/2 Stars, Top Pick!
"A romance of rare depth,
humor and sensuality."
—*Romantic Times* BOOKclub on
*Beauty and the Black Sheep*

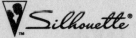

# COMING NEXT MONTH

**SPECIAL EDITION**

**#1729 PRODIGAL SON—Susan Mallery**
*Family Business*
After his father's death, it was up to eldest son Jack Hanson to save
the troubled family business. Hiring his beautiful business school
rival Samantha Edwards helped—her creative ideas worked wonders.
But her unorthodox style rankled by-the-books Jack. They were
headed for an office showdown...*and* falling for each other behind
closed doors.

**#1730 A PERFECT LIFE—Patricia Kay**
*Callie's Corner Café*
The divorce was tough enough on Shawn Fletcher—selling the house
and watching her ex remarry *really* stung. So a flirtation with her
daughter's math teacher, Matt McFarland, came as a nice surprise.
But when things with the younger man seemed serious, Shawn
panicked—how would her daughter and the Callie's Corner Café
gang take the news?

**#1731 HIS MOTHER'S WEDDING—Judy Duarte**
Private eye Rico Garcia blamed his cynicism about romance on
his mom, who after four marriages had found a "soul mate"—again!
Rico's help with the new wedding put him on a collision course
with gorgeous, Pollyanna-ish wedding planner Molly Townsend.
The attraction sizzled...but was it enough to melt the detective's
world-weary veneer?

**#1732 HIS COMFORT AND JOY—Jessica Bird**
*The Moorehouse Legacy*
For dress designer Joy Moorehouse, July and August were the kindest
months—when brash politico Gray Bennett summered in
her hometown of Saranac. She innocently admired him from afar until
things between them took a sudden turn. Soon work led Joy
to Gray's Manhattan stomping ground...and passions escalated in
a New York minute.

**#1733 THE THREE-WAY MIRACLE—Karen Sandler**
Devoted to managing the Rescued Hearts Riding School,
Sara Rand kept men at arm's length, and volunteer building contractor
Keith Delacroix was no exception. But then Sara and Keith had to join
forces to find a missing student. Looking for
the little girl made them reflect on loss and abuse in their pasts,
and mutual attraction in the present....

**#1734 THE DOCTOR'S SECRET CHILD—Kate Welsh**
CEO Caroline Hopewell knew heartbreak. Her father had died,
leaving her to raise his son by a second marriage, and the boy
had a rare illness. Then Caroline discovered the truth: the child wasn't
her father's. But the endearing attentions of the true dad,
Dr. Trey Westerly, for his newfound child stirred Caroline's soul...
giving her hope for the future.